FRANÇOISE SAGAN

Bonjour Tristesse and
A Certain Smile

With an Introduction by Rachel Cusk
Translated by Irene Ash

PENGUIN BOOKS

PENGUIN CLASSICS

Published by the Penguin Group
Penguin Books Ltd, 80 Strand, London WC2R ORL, England
Penguin Group (USA) Inc., 375 Hudson Street, New York, New York 10014, USA
Penguin Group (Canada), 90 Eglinton Avenue East, Suite 700, Toronto, Ontario,
Canada M4P 2Y3 (a division of Pearson Penguin Canada Inc.)
Penguin Ireland, 25 St Stephen's Green, Dublin 2, Ireland
(a division of Penguin Books Ltd)
Penguin Group (Australia), 250 Camberwell Road, Camberwell, Victoria 3124, Australia
(a division of Pearson Australia Group Pty Ltd)
Penguin Books India Pvt Ltd, 11 Community Centre, Panchsheel Park,
New Delhi – 110 017, India
Penguin Group (NZ), 67 Apollo Drive, Rosedale, North Shore 0632, New Zealand
(a division of Pearson New Zealand Ltd)
Penguin Books (South Africa) (Pty) Ltd, 24 Sturdee Avenue, Rosebank, Johannesburg
2196, South Africa

Penguin Books Ltd, Registered Offices: 80 Strand, London WC2R ORL, England

www.penguin.co

Bonjour Tristesse f
First published in
Published in Pen;
A Certain Smile fir
First published in
Published in Pen;
This edition first
2

Copyright © The
Introduction cop
All rights reserve

The moral right

Typeset by Palimpsest Book Production Limited, Grangemouth, Stirlingshire
Printed in England by Clays Ltd, St Ives plc

ISBN 978-0-141-44230-3

www.greenpenguin.co.uk

Contents

Introduction by Rachel Cusk 1

BONJOUR TRISTESSE 9
A CERTAIN SMILE 111

Introduction

New readers are warned that the introduction reveals details of the plot.

It is one of the ironies of the writer's predicament that self-expression can sometimes become fate. The fiction lays a fetter on the life. To the reader, as often as not, it will all seem to be part of the same story. Scott Fitzgerald, for instance, virtually described his own funeral in *The Great Gatsby*. Albert Camus, more eerily, foretold precisely the manner of his death in *La Chute*. Vaguely, the reader comes to see the writer as nothing more than one of his on her own characters: the suspicion that literature occurs entirely within the bounds of personality is confirmed. A kind of disappointment afflicts our feelings about writers, as it does not those about other artists. It is as though they, with their mortal grasp on the faculty of imagination, have crushed our illusions about human destiny. They have described existence, but they have failed to transcend it. They have failed to provide us with a happy ending.

The obituaries that followed Françoise Sagan's death in 2004 were full of the sense of this failure. She had become, we were told, a tragic, pitiable figure: destitute, isolated, tainted by scandal and alcoholism. She had, of course, produced many books, but none as successful and hence as troubling to history as her first, published when she was just nineteen. In that book, *Bonjour Tristesse*, she described the hedonism and amorality of youth, the hedonism and amorality of well-heeled French intellectuals, the hedonism and amorality of post-war Europe on the cusp of the sixties. Not surprisingly, it was the hedonism and the amorality of her life that interested the obituary-writers. For there it was, her fetter, her fate: from this slender, misunderstood novel, and from its young heroine Céline, Françoise Sagan never escaped. *Bonjour Tristesse* concludes with a fatal car accident, and three years after its publication Sagan, whose love of dangerous driving invariably forms part of the legend of her life, received severe head injuries when her Aston Martin crashed at high speed. The disappointment among the obituary-writers that the author did not submit then and there to her fictional destiny is palpable.

If there is hedonism, if there is amorality in *Bonjour Tristesse*, then it is of a most artistically proper kind. Morality, and its absence, is the novel's defining theme: in this sense Sagan is far more of a classicist than her Existentialist brethren Sartre and Camus. Certainly, she concerns herself with the twentieth-century problem of personal reality, of the self and its interaction with behavioural norms, but in *Bonjour Tristesse* those norms are as much psychical as societal. Céline, a motherless seventeen-year-old whose permissive, feckless father has provided the only yardstick for her values and personal conduct, offers Sagan a particularly naked example of the human sensibility taking shape. Céline's encounters with questions of right and wrong, and with the way those questions cut across her physical and emotional desires, constitute an interrogation of morality that it is difficult to credit as the work of an eighteen-year-old author. What is the moral sense? Where does it come from? Is it necessary? Is it intrinsic to human nature? Is it possible to lack a moral sense, and if so does that discredit morality itself? These are the questions that lie at the heart of this brief and disturbing novel.

Céline and her father, Raymond, have decided to rent a summer villa on the Côte d'Azur for two months. Raymond is bringing his girlfriend, Elsa, along for the holiday, though Céline is anxious that the reader should not disapprove: 'I must explain this situation at once, or it might give a false impression. My father was forty, and had been a widower for fifteen years.' Notice that it is Raymond who has been bereaved, not Céline herself: she tells us only that she had been at boarding school until two years earlier. Later, she remembers her father's embarrassment at her ugly uniform and plaited hair when he came to collect her from the station. It is as though they had not seen each other in the intervening years; as though Céline, between the ages of two and fifteen, was an orphan. 'And then in the car his sudden triumphant joy because I had his eyes, his mouth, and I was going to be for him the dearest, most marvellous of toys.'

At the villa the trio are contentedly idle. They swim and sunbathe; they are untroubled by the sense of duty or compunction. Raymond does beach exercises to diminish his belly. The beautiful, vapid, red-haired Elsa badly burns her skin. Céline, who has recently failed her exams at the Sorbonne, lies on the beach running sand through her fingers: 'I told myself that it ran out like time. It was an idle thought, and it was pleasant to have idle thoughts, for it was summer.' One day, a young man capsizes his sailing boat in their creek – this is Cyril, an ardent, good-looking, conventional university student who offers to teach Céline how to sail, and is the ideal prospect for a summer romance.

Chance, impulse, happenstance: this is how life unfolds in the unexamined world of Raymond and Céline. They do not concern themselves with order and structure, the imposition of the will, the resistance to certain desires and the aspiration towards certain goals. Even Elsa merely submits to the sun's power to burn her. Is this the correct way to live? The question does not arise; there is no one to ask it. Until, that is, Raymond announces one evening that he has invited a woman named Anne Larsen to stay. The first thing we learn about Anne is that she was a friend of Céline's dead mother. With the mother, the whole lost world of order, nurture and morality is powerfully invoked. Anne, it is clear, is the emissary of that world: 'I knew that once she had come it would be impossible for any of us to relax completely,' says Céline. 'Anne gave a shape to things and a meaning to words that my father and I prefer to ignore. She set a standard of good taste and fastidiousness which one could not help noticing in her sudden withdrawals, her expressions, and her pained silences.' Anne is beautiful, sophisticated, successful; and unlike Céline, Raymond and Elsa, she is an adult, with an adult's power of censure and moral judgement.

Cyril, too, is an adult – he is shocked by Raymond and Elsa's ménage, and apologizes to Céline for kissing her. 'You have no protection against me . . . I might be the most awful cad for all you know,' he says, in a most uncad-like way. When Anne arrives, it is clear that she means to take Raymond and Céline in hand. It is clear, too, that she is in love with Raymond, and that Raymond has reached for her in a bid to escape the pleasurable anomie of his circumstances and the childlike emotional world that he inhabits with Céline. Elsa is dispatched; the mature, glacial, controlling Anne is installed. Soon she and Raymond announce their plans to marry; immediately, Anne begins to impose her will on Céline. She orders her to eat more, to study in her room instead of going to the beach, to cease outright her relations with Cyril. Is this love or is it hatred? Is it nurture or is it control? Is it common sense, or the jealousy of a constricted older woman for her uninhibited stepdaughter? Is it what Céline has missed out on by not having a mother of her own, or what her motherlessness has exposed her to?

Sagan records clearly the effect the change in regime has on Céline: 'It was for this I reproached Anne: she prevented me from liking myself. I . . . had been forced by her into a world of self-criticism and guilty conscience . . . For the first time in my life I was divided against myself.' In one sense, then, morality is a form of self-hatred; it is a wound one assuages by wounding others in precisely the same way. But Anne has done something else – she has stolen Céline's father, her one source of unconditional love. Raymond is now 'estranged' from his daughter; he has 'disarmed and abandoned' her. Céline the divided girl is forced into immorality: she wishes to get rid of Anne and regain Raymond. Her actual powerlessness gives rise to fantasies of power, and these thoughts cause her to oscillate between hatred and terrible guilt. Here, then, is another indictment of morality, as it is lived by Anne. Anne has fomented violence in Céline's pacific nature. By controlling and censuring her, and by interfering with her source of love, she has given her the capacity to do wrong.

This is a masterly portrait of primal human bonds and needs that cannot but be read as a critique of family life, the treatment of children, and the psychical consequences of different forms of upbringing. One day, Anne locks Céline in her room, after an argument about schoolwork. At first Céline panics, and flings herself at the door like a wild animal. 'It was my first experience of cruelty.' Then her heart is hardened, her duplicity sealed: 'I sat on my bed and began to plan my revenge.' The form this revenge takes occupies the final section of the book, and is almost theatrical in its psychological grandeur. Céline chooses as her tools her father's childishness, Anne's intransigence, Elsa's vanity, Cyril's responsible nature, and with them she forges a plot in which each of the four is utterly at her mercy. As a dramatist she experiences, for the first time, complete power over others. Her plot is tragic and bitter, but it plays uninterrupted to its end. Neither right nor wrong, neither conformity nor permissiveness, neither love nor hatred winds up the victor of this moral battle: it is insight, the writer's greatest gift, that wins.

Sagan's second novel, *A Certain Smile*, is in many ways a sequel to *Bonjour Tristesse*. Several of the familiar themes are there: the search for and betrayal of the lost mother; the double nature of father/lover and lover/brother; the defence of boredom or nothingness as a moral position more truthful than conventionality. Dominique, a law student at the Sorbonne, meets Luc, the married uncle of her boyfriend, Bertrand. Luc and his gentle, kindly wife, Françoise, take Dominique under their wing, for she is uncared-for and alone, the daughter of distant provincial parents rendered more remote by their unassuageable grief over the death some years earlier of 'a son', as Dominique expresses it. Like Céline, Dominique struggles to maintain the dignity of her own reality, to assert its truth, however abnormal other people might claim to find it. 'I was contented enough, but there was always a part of myself, warm and alive, that longed for tears, solitude, and excitement.'

Luc quickly begins to made advances towards Dominique, even as Françoise is enveloping her in mother-love. Dominique profits from their attention, but can find no moral path through it, for the two forms of affection – sexual and parental – are confused. Luc proposes that Dominique come away with him and have a brief affair, at the end of which he will return to Françoise. Once again, the father-figure is identified with an aberrant morality that results in the girl's betrayal of the mother-figure. More importantly, he denies her emotional reality: according to Luc, his affair with Dominique can proceed only on the basis that she does not love him. The nature of love is the novel's central preoccupation. The uncanny maturity that made Sagan's name as a novelist is most strongly in evidence in her fearless and astute portrayal of love as a psychical event that has its roots in family life and the early formation of personality. To the modern reader, Luc's conduct towards Dominique has strong undercurrents of abuse: her violent emotional trauma in the aftermath of the affair, and the novel's exquisitely ambivalent ending in which the subjective death and rebirth of Dominique is described, go far beyond poignancy or even frankness. 'Something is rotten in the state of Denmark!' Dominique finds herself repeating, without knowing why. Sagan's sense of emotional tragedy is indeed that of the great dramatists.

'Much of the time life is a sort of rhythmic progression of three characters,' Sagan said in an interview, shortly before the publication of *A Certain Smile*. In *Bonjour Tristesse*, this structural tenet is illustrated almost sculpturally by Céline's description of the three adults standing on the stairs the night Raymond transfers his affections from Elsa to Anne: 'I remember the scene perfectly. First of all, in front of me, Anne's golden neck and perfect shoulders, a little lower down my father's fascinated face and extended hand, and, already in the distance, Elsa's silhouette.' These two novels, so spare and rigorous, so artistically correct, so thorough in their psychological realism, are the highest expression of the triangular purity of their author's strange and beautiful *esthétique*.

Rachel Cusk

Bonjour Tristesse

Adieu tristesse
Bonjour tristesse
Tu es inscrite dans les lignes du plafond
Tu es inscrite dans les yeux que j'aime
Tu n'es pas tout a fait la misère
Car les lèvres les plus pauvres te dénoncent
Par un sourire
Bonjour tristesse
Amour des corps aimables
Puissance de l'amour
Dont l'amabilité surgit
Comme un monstre sans corps
Tête désappointée
Tristesse beau visage.

PAUL ÉLUARD
'À peine défigurée', La vie immédiate

PART ONE

I

A strange melancholy pervades me to which I hesitate to give the grave and beautiful name of sadness. In the past the idea of sadness always appealed to me, now I am almost ashamed of its complete egoism. I had known boredom, regret, and at times remorse, but never sadness. Today something envelops me like a silken web, enervating and soft, which isolates me.

That summer I was seventeen and perfectly happy. I lived with my father, and there was also Elsa, who for the time being was his mistress. I must explain this situation at once, or it might give a false impression. My father was forty, and had been a widower for fifteen years. He was young for his age, full of vitality and possibilities, and when I left school two years before, I soon noticed that he lived with a woman. It took me rather longer to realize that it was a different one every six months. But gradually his charm, my new easy life, and my own disposition led me to accept it. He was a frivolous man, clever at business, always curious, quickly bored, and attractive to women. It was easy to love him, for he was kind, generous, gay, and full of affection for me. I cannot imagine a better or a more amusing friend. At the beginning of the summer he even went so far as to ask me whether I would object to Elsa's company during the holidays. She was a tall red-haired girl, sensual and worldly, gentle, rather simple, and unpretentious; one might have come across her any day in the studios and bars of the Champs-Élysées. I encouraged

him to invite her. He needed women around him, and I knew
that Elsa would not get in our way. In any case my father and
I were so delighted at the prospect of going away together that
we were in no mood to cavil at anything. He had rented a large
white villa on the Mediterranean, for which we had been longing
since the spring. It was remote and beautiful, and stood on a
promontory dominating the sea, hidden from the road by a pine
wood; a mule path led down to a tiny creek where the sea lapped
against rust-coloured rocks.

The first days were dazzling. We spent hours on the beach overwhelmed by the heat and gradually assuming a healthy golden tan;
except Elsa, whose skin reddened and peeled, causing her atrocious
suffering. My father performed all sorts of complicated leg exercises
to reduce a rounding stomach unsuitable for a Don Juan. From
dawn onwards I was in the water. It was cool and transparent and I
plunged wildly about in my efforts to wash away the shadows and
dust of the city. I lay full length on the sand, took up a handful and
let it run through my fingers in soft yellow streams. I told myself
that it ran out like time. It was an idle thought, and it was pleasant
to have idle thoughts, for it was summer.

On the sixth day I saw Cyril. He was sailing a small boat which
capsized in front of our creek. We had a good deal of fun rescu-
ing his possessions, during which he told me his name, that he
was studying law, and was spending his holidays with his mother
in a neighbouring villa. He looked typically Latin, and was very
dark and sunburnt. There was something reliable and protective
about him which I liked at once. Usually I avoided university
students, whom I considered rough, and only interested in themselves and their own problems, which they dramatized, or used
as an excuse for their boredom. I did not care for young people,
I much preferred my father's friends, men of forty, who spoke
to me with courtesy and tenderness, and treated me with the
gentleness of a father or a lover.

But Cyril was different. He was tall and sometimes beautiful, with the sort of good looks that immediately inspire one with confidence. Although I did not share my father's aversion to ugliness, which often led us to associate with stupid people, I felt vaguely uncomfortable with anyone devoid of physical charms. Their resignation to the fact that they were unattractive seemed to me somehow indecent.

When Cyril left he offered to teach me to sail. I went up to dinner absorbed by my thoughts and hardly joined in the conversation; neither did I pay much attention to my father's nervousness. After dinner we lay in chairs on the terrace as usual. The sky was studded with stars. I gazed upwards, vaguely hoping to see a sudden, exciting flash across the heavens, but it was early in July and too soon for meteors. On the terrace the crickets were chirruping. There must have been thousands of them, drunk with heat and moonlight, pouring out their strange song all night long. I had been told they were only rubbing their wing-cases together, but I preferred to believe that it came from the throat, guttural and instinctive like the purr of a cat. We were very comfortable. Only some tiny grains of sand between my skin and my shirt kept me from dropping off to sleep. Suddenly my father coughed apologetically and sat up.

'Someone is coming to stay,' he announced.

I shut my eyes tightly. We were too peaceful, it just couldn't last!

'Hurry up and tell us who it is!' cried Elsa, always avid for gossip.

'Anne Larsen,' said my father and he turned towards me.

I could hardly believe my ears. Anne was the last person I would have thought of. She had been a friend of my mother's, and had very little connection with my father. But all the same, when I left school two years before and my father was at his wits' end about me, he had asked her to take me in hand. Within a week she had dressed me in the right clothes and taught me something of life. I remember thinking her the most wonderful person and being quite embarrassingly fond of her, but she soon found me a young man to whom I could transfer my affections. To her I owed my first glimpse of elegance and my first flirtation, and I was very grateful. At forty-two she was a most attractive woman, much sought after, with a beautiful face, proud, tired, and indifferent. This indifference was the only complaint one could make against her: she was amiable and distant. Everything about her denoted a strong will and an inner serenity which were disconcerting. Although divorced, she seemed to have no attachments; but then we did not know the same people. Her friends were clever, intelligent and discreet; ours, from whom my father demanded only good looks or amusement, were noisy and insatiable. I think she rather despised us for our love of diversion and frivolity, as she despised all extremes. We had few points of contact: she was concerned with fashion and my father with publicity, so they met occasionally at business dinners; then there was the memory of my mother, and lastly my own determined efforts to keep in touch, because although she intimidated me, I greatly admired her. In short, her sudden arrival appeared disastrous in view of Elsa's presence and Anne's ideas on education.

Elsa went up to bed after making close enquiries about Anne's social position. I remained alone with my father and moved to the steps, where I sat at his feet. He leaned forward and laid his hands on my shoulders.

'Why are you so upset, darling? You look like a little wild cat. I'd rather have a beautiful fair-haired daughter, a bit plump, with china-blue eyes and . . .'

'That's hardly the point,' I said. 'What made you invite Anne, and why did she accept?'

'Perhaps she wants to see your old father, one never knows.'

'You're not the type of man who interests Anne,' I said. 'She's too intelligent and thinks too much of herself. And what about Elsa, have you thought of her? Can you imagine a conversation between Elsa and Anne? I can't!'

'I'm afraid it hadn't occurred to me,' he confessed. 'But you're right, it's a dreadful thought! Cécile, my sweet, shall we go back to Paris?'

He laughed softly and rubbed the back of my neck. I turned to look at him. His dark eyes gleamed, funny little wrinkles marked their edges, his mouth turned up slightly. He looked like a faun. I laughed with him as I always did when he created complications for himself.

'My little accomplice,' he said. 'What would I do without you?'

From the tender inflection of his voice I knew that he would have really been unhappy. Late into the night we talked of love, of its complications. In my father's eyes they were imaginary. He refused categorically all notions of fidelity and serious commitments. He explained that they were arbitrary and sterile. From anyone else such views would have shocked me, but I knew that in his case they did not exclude either tenderness or devotion; feelings which came all the more easily to him since he was determined that they should be transient. This conception of rapid, violent and passing love affairs appealed to my imagination. I was not at the age when fidelity is attractive. I knew very little about love.

2

Anne was not due for another week, and I made the most of these last days of real freedom. We had rented the villa for two months, but I knew that once she had come it would be impossible for any of us to relax completely. Anne gave a shape to things and a meaning to words that my father and I prefer to ignore. She set a standard of good taste and fastidiousness which one could not help noticing in her sudden withdrawals, her expressions, and her pained silences. It was both stimulating and exhausting, but in the long run humiliating, because I could not help feeling that she was right.

On the day of her arrival we decided that my father and Elsa should meet her at the station in Fréjus. I absolutely refused to go with them. In desperation my father cut all the gladioli in the garden to offer her as soon as she got off the train. My only advice to him was not to allow Elsa to carry the bouquet. After they had left I went down to the beach. It was three o'clock and the heat was overpowering. I was lying on the sand half asleep when I heard Cyril's voice. I opened my eyes: the sky was white, shimmering with heat. I made no reply, because I did not want to speak to him, nor to anyone. I was nailed to the sand by all the forces of summer.

'Are you dead?' he said. 'From over there you looked as if you had been washed up by the sea.'

I smiled. He sat down near me and my heart began to beat

faster because his hand had just touched my shoulder. A dozen times during the past week my brilliant seamanship had precipitated us into the water, our arms entwined, and I had not felt the least twinge of excitement, but today the heat, my half-sleep, and an inadvertent movement had somehow broken down my defences. We looked at each other. I was getting to know him better. He was steady, and more restrained than is perhaps usual at his age. For this reason our circumstances – our unusual trio – shocked him. He was too kind or too timid to tell me, but I felt it in the oblique looks of recrimination he gave my father. He would have liked to know that I was tormented by our situation, but I was not; in fact my only torment at that moment was the way my heart was thumping. He bent over me. I thought of the past few days, of my feeling of peace and confidence when I was with him, and I regretted the approach of that wide and rather full mouth.

'Cyril,' I said. 'We were so happy . . .'

He kissed me gently. I looked at the sky, then saw nothing but lights bursting under my closed eyelids. The warmth, dizziness, and the taste of our first kisses continued for long moments. The sound of a motorhorn separated us like thieves. I left Cyril without a word and went up to the house. I was surprised by their quick return; Anne's train could hardly have arrived yet. Nevertheless I found her on the terrace just getting out of a car.

'This is like the house of the Sleeping Beauty!' she said. 'How brown you are, Cécile! I am so pleased to see you.'

'I too,' I answered, 'but have you just come from Paris?'

'I preferred to drive down, and by the way, I'm worn out.'

I showed her to her room and opened the window in the hope of seeing Cyril's boat, but it had disappeared. Anne sat down on the bed. I noticed little shadows round her eyes.

'What a delightful villa!' she said. 'Where's the master of the house?'

'He's gone to meet you at the station with Elsa.'

I had put her suitcase on a chair, and when I turned round I received a shock. Her face had suddenly collapsed, her mouth was trembling.

'Elsa Mackenbourg? He brought Elsa Mackenbourg here?'

I could not think of anything to reply. I looked at her, absolutely stupefied. Was that really the face I had always seen so calm and controlled? . . . She stared at me, but I saw she was contemplating my words. When at last she noticed me she turned her head away.

'I ought to have let you know sooner,' she said, 'but I was in such a hurry to get away and so tired.'

'And now . . .' I continued mechanically.

'Now what?' she said.

Her expression was interrogatory, disdainful, as though nothing had taken place.

'Well, now you've arrived!' I said stupidly, rubbing my hands together. 'You can't think how pleased I am that you're here. I'll wait for you downstairs; if you'd like anything to drink the bar is very well stocked.'

Talking incoherently I left the room and went downstairs with my thoughts in a turmoil. What was the reason for that expression, that worried voice, that sudden despondency? I sat on the sofa and closed my eyes. I tried to remember Anne's various faces: hard, reassuring; her expressions of irony, ease, authority. I found myself both moved and irritated by the discovery that she was vulnerable. Was she in love with my father? Was it possible for her to be in love? He was not at all her type. He was weak, frivolous, and sometimes unreliable. But perhaps it was only the fatigue of the journey, or moral indignation? I spent an hour in vain conjecture.

At five o'clock my father arrived with Elsa. I watched him getting out of the car. I wondered if Anne could ever love him. He walked quickly towards me, his head tilted a little backwards;

he smiled. Of course it was quite possible for Anne to love him, for anyone to love him!

'Anne wasn't there,' he called to me. 'I hope she hasn't fallen out of the train!'

'She's in her room,' I said. 'She came in her car.'

'No? Splendid! Then all you have to do is to take up the bouquet.'

'Did you buy me some flowers?' called Anne's voice. 'How sweet of you!'

She came down the stairs to meet him, cool, smiling, in a dress that did not seem to have travelled. I reflected sadly how she had appeared only when she heard the car, and that she might have done so a little sooner to talk to me; even if it had been about my examination, in which, by the way, I had failed. This last thought consoled me.

My father rushed up to her and kissed her hand.

'I spent a quarter of an hour on the station platform, holding this bunch of flowers, and feeling utterly foolish. Thank goodness you're here! Do you know Elsa Mackenbourg?'

I averted my eyes.

'We must have met,' said Anne, all amiability. 'What a lovely room I have. It was most kind of you to invite me, Raymond; I was feeling very exhausted.'

My father gave a snort of pleasure. In his eyes everything was going well. He made conversation, uncorked bottles; but I kept thinking, first of Cyril's passionate face, and then of Anne's, both with the stamp of violence on them, and I wondered if the holidays would be as uncomplicated as my father had predicted.

This first dinner was very gay. My father and Anne talked of the friends they had in common, who were few, but highly colourful. I was enjoying myself up to the moment when Anne declared that my father's business partner was an idiot. He was a

23

man who drank a lot, but I liked him very much, and my father and I had had memorable meals in his company.

'But Anne,' I protested. 'Lombard is most amusing; he can even be very funny.'

'All the same, you must admit that he's somewhat lacking, and as for his brand of humour . . .'

'He has perhaps not a very brilliant form of intelligence, but . . .'

She interrupted me with an air of condescension:

'What you call "forms" of intelligence are only degrees.'

I was delighted with her clear-cut definition. Certain phrases fascinate me with their subtle implications, even though I may not always understand their meaning. I told Anne that I wished I could have written it down in my notebook. My father burst out laughing:

'At least you bear no resentment!'

How could I when Anne was not malevolent? I felt that she was too completely indifferent, her judgements had not the precision, the sharp edge of spite, and so were all the more effective.

The first evening Anne did not seem to notice that Elsa went quite openly into my father's bedroom. She had brought me a jersey from her collection, but would not accept any thanks; it only bored her to be thanked, she said, and as I was anyhow shy of expressing enthusiasm, I was most relieved.

'I think Elsa is very nice,' she remarked as I was about to leave the room.

She looked straight at me without a smile, seeking something in me which at all cost she wished to eradicate: I was to forget her earlier reaction.

'Oh yes, she's a charming girl . . . very *sympathique*,' I stammered.

She began to laugh, and I went up to bed, most upset. I fell asleep thinking of Cyril, probably dancing in Cannes with girls.

I realize that I have forgotten an important factor – the presence of the sea with its incessant rhythm. Neither have I remembered the four lime trees in the courtyard of a school in Provence, and their scent; and my father's smile on the station platform three years ago when I left school, his embarrassed smile because I had plaits and wore an ugly dark dress. And then in the car his sudden triumphant joy because I had his eyes, his mouth, and I was going to be for him the dearest, most marvellous of toys. I knew nothing; he was going to show me Paris, luxury, the easy life. I dare say I owed most of my pleasures of that time to money; the pleasure of driving fast, of having a new dress, buying records, books, flowers. Even now I am not ashamed of indulging in these pleasures, in fact I just take them for granted. I would rather deny myself my moods of mysticism or despair than give them up. My love of pleasure seems to be the only coherent side of my character. Perhaps it is because I have not read enough? At school one only reads edifying works. In Paris there was no time for reading: after lectures my friends hurried me off to cinemas; they were surprised to find that I did not even know the actors' names. I sat on sunny café terraces, I savoured the pleasure of drifting along with the crowds, of having a drink, of being with someone who looks into your eyes, holds your hand, and then leads you far away from those same crowds. We would walk slowly home, there under a doorway he would draw me close and embrace me: I found out how pleasant it was to be kissed. In the evenings I grew older: I went to parties with my father. They were very mixed parties, and I was rather out of place, but I enjoyed myself, and the fact that I was so young seemed to amuse everyone. When we left, my father would drop me at our flat, and then see his friend home. I never heard him come in.

I do not want to give the impression that he was vain about his affairs, but he made no effort to hide them from me, or to

invent stories in order to justify the frequent presence at breakfast of a particular friend, not even if she became a member
of our household (fortunately only temporarily!). In any case I
would soon have discovered the nature of his relations with his
'guests', and probably he found it easier to be frank than to take
the trouble to deceive me, and thereby lose my confidence. His
only fault was to imbue me with a cynical attitude towards love
which, considering my age and experience, should have meant
happiness and not only a transitory sensation. I was fond of
repeating to myself sayings like Oscar Wilde's:

Sin is the only note of vivid colour that persists in the modern world.

I made it my own with far more conviction, I think, than if I had
put it into practice. I believed that I could base my life on it.

3

The next morning I was awakened by a slanting ray of hot sunshine that flooded my bed and put an end to my strange and rather confused dreams. Still half asleep I raised my hand to shield my face from the insistent heat, then gave it up. It was ten o'clock. I went down to the terrace in my pyjamas and found Anne glancing through the newspapers. I noticed that she was lightly, but perfectly, made up; apparently she never allowed herself a real holiday. As she paid no attention to me, I sat down on the steps with a cup of coffee and an orange to enjoy the delicious morning. I bit the orange and let its sweet juice run into my mouth, then took a gulp of scalding black coffee and went back to the orange again. The sun warmed my hair and smoothed away the marks of the sheet on my skin. I thought in five minutes I would go and bathe. Anne's voice made me jump:

'Cécile, aren't you eating anything?'

'I prefer just a drink in the morning.'

'To look presentable you ought to put on six pounds; your cheeks are hollow and one can count every rib. Do go in and fetch yourself some bread and butter!'

I begged her not to force me to eat, and she was just explaining how important it was when my father appeared in his sumptuous spotted dressing-gown.

'What a charming spectacle,' he said, 'two little girls sunning themselves and discussing bread and butter.'

'Unfortunately there's only one little girl,' said Anne, laughing. 'I'm your age, my dear Raymond!'

'Caustic as ever!' he said gently, and I saw Anne's eyelids flutter as if she had received an unexpected caress.

I slipped away unnoticed. On the stairs I passed Elsa. She was obviously just out of bed, with swollen eyelids, pale lips, and her skin crimson from too much sun. I almost stopped her to say that Anne was downstairs, her face trim and immaculate; that *she* would be careful to tan slowly and without damage. I nearly put her on her guard, but probably she would have taken it badly: she was twenty-nine, thirteen years younger than Anne, and that seemed to her a master trump.

I fetched my bathing suit and ran to the creek. To my surprise Cyril was already there, sitting on his boat. He came to meet me looking serious and took my hands.

'I wanted to beg your pardon for yesterday,' he said.

'It was my fault,' I replied, wondering why he was so solemn.

'I'm very annoyed with myself,' he went on, pushing the boat into the water.

'There's no reason to be,' I said lightly.

'But I am!'

I was already in the boat. He was standing in the water up to his knees, resting his hands on the gunwale as if it were the bar of a tribunal. I knew his face well enough to read his expression and realized that he would not join me until he had said what was on his mind. It made me laugh to think that at twenty-five he saw himself as a seducer.

'Don't laugh,' he said, 'I really meant it. You have no protection against me. Look at the example of your father and that woman! I might be the most awful cad for all you know.'

He was not at all ridiculous. I thought he was kind, already half in love with me, and that it would be nice to be in love with him too. I put my arm around his neck and my cheek against his. He had broad shoulders and his body felt hard against mine.

'You're very sweet, Cyril,' I murmured. 'You shall be a brother to me.'

He folded his arm round me with an angry little exclamation, and gently pulled me out of the boat. He held me close against him, my head on his shoulders. At that moment I loved him. In the morning light he was as golden, as soft, as gentle as myself. He was protecting me. As his lips touched mine we both began to tremble, and the pleasure of our kiss was untinged by shame or regret, merely a deep searching interrupted every now and then by whispers. I broke away and swam towards the boat, which was drifting out. I dipped my face into the water to refresh it. The water was green. A feeling of reckless happiness came over me.

At half past eleven Cyril left, and my father and his women appeared on the mule path. He walked between the two, supporting them, offering his hand to each in turn with a charm and naturalness all his own. Anne had kept on her beach wrap. She removed it with complete unconcern, while we all watched her, and lay down on the sand. She had a small waist and perfect legs, and, no doubt as the result of a lifetime of care and attention, her body was almost without a blemish. Involuntarily I glanced at my father, raising an eyebrow of approval. To my great surprise he did not respond, but closed his eyes. Poor Elsa, who was in a lamentable condition, was busy oiling herself. I did not think my father would stand her for another week . . . Anne turned her head towards me:

'Cécile, why do you get up so early here? In Paris you stayed in bed until midday.'

'I was working,' I said. 'It made my legs ache.'

She did not smile. She only smiled when she felt like it, never out of politeness, like other people.

'And your exam?'

'Ploughed!' I said brightly. 'Well and truly ploughed.'

'But you *must* pass it in October.'

'Why should she?' my father interrupted. 'I never got any diplomas and I live a life of luxury.'

'You had quite a fortune to start with,' Anne reminded him.

'My daughter will always find men to look after her,' said my father grandiloquently.

Elsa began to laugh, but stopped when she saw our three faces.

'She will have to work during the holidays,' said Anne, shutting her eyes to put an end to the conversation.

I gave my father a despairing look, but he merely smiled sheepishly. I saw myself in front of an open page of Bergson, its black lines dancing before my eyes, while Cyril was laughing outside. The idea horrified me. I crawled over to Anne and called her in a low voice. She opened her eyes. I bent an anxious, pleading face over her, drawing in my cheeks to make myself look like an overworked intellectual.

'Anne,' I said, 'you're not going to do that to me, make me work in this heat . . . these holidays could do me so much good.'

She stared at me for a moment, then smiled mysteriously and turned her head away.

'I shall have to make you do "that", even in this heat, as you say. You'll be angry with me for a day or two, as I know you, but you'll pass your exam.'

'There are things one cannot be made to do,' I said grimly.

Her only response was a supercilious look, and I returned to my place full of foreboding. Elsa was chattering about various festivities along the Riviera, but my father was not listening. From his place at the apex of the triangle formed by their bodies, he was gazing at Anne's upturned profile with a resolute stare that I recognized. His hand opened and closed on the sand with a gentle, regular, persistent movement. I ran down to the sea and plunged in, bemoaning the holiday we might have had. All the elements of a drama were to hand: a seducer, a demi-mondaine and a determined woman. I saw an exquisite red and blue shell on the sea-bed. I dived for it, and held it, smooth and empty, in my hand all the morning. I decided it was a lucky charm, and that I would keep it. I am surprised that I have not lost it, for I lose everything. Today it is still pink and warm as it lies in my palm, and makes me feel like crying.

4

Anne was extraordinarily kind to Elsa during the following days. In spite of the numerous silly remarks that punctuated Elsa's conversation, she never gave vent to any of those cutting phrases which were her speciality, and which would have covered the poor girl with ridicule. I was most surprised, and began to admire Anne's forbearance and generosity without realizing how subtle she was; for my father, who would soon have tired of such cruel tactics, was now filled with gratitude towards her. He used his appreciation as a pretext for drawing her, so to speak, into the family circle; by implying all the time that I was partly her responsibility, and altogether behaving towards her as if she were a second mother to me. But I noticed that his every look and gesture betrayed a secret desire for her. Whenever I caught a similar gleam in Cyril's eye, it left me undecided whether to egg him on or to run away. On that point I must have been more easily influenced than Anne, for her attitude to my father expressed such indifference and calm friendliness that I was reassured. I began to believe that I had been mistaken the first day. I did not notice that this unconcern of hers was just what provoked my father. And then there were her silences, apparently so artless and full of fine feeling, and such a contrast to Elsa's incessant chatter, that it was like light and shade. Poor Elsa! She had really no suspicions whatsoever, and although still suffering from the effects of the sun, remained her usual talkative and exuberant self.

A day came, however, when she must have intercepted a look

of my father's and drawn her own conclusions from it. Before lunch I saw her whispering into his ear. For a moment he seemed rather put out, but then he nodded and smiled. After coffee Elsa walked over to the door, turned round, and striking a languorous, film-star pose, said in an affected voice:

'Are you coming, Raymond?'

My father got up and followed her, muttering something about the benefits of the siesta. Anne had not moved, her cigarette was smouldering between her fingers. I felt I ought to say something.

'People say that a siesta is restful, but I think it is the opposite . . .'

I stopped short, conscious that my words were equivocal.

'That's enough,' said Anne dryly.

There was nothing equivocal about her tone. She had of course found my remark in bad taste, but when I looked at her I saw that her face was deliberately calm and composed. It made me feel that perhaps at that moment she was passionately jealous of Elsa. While I was wondering how I could console her, a cynical idea occurred to me. Cynicism always enchanted me by producing a delicious feeling of self-assurance and of being in league with myself. I could not keep it back:

'I imagine that with Elsa's sunburn that kind of siesta can't be very exciting for either of them.'

I would have done better to say nothing.

'I detest that kind of remark. At your age it's not only stupid, but deplorable.'

I suddenly felt angry:

'I only said it as a joke, you know. I'm sure they are really quite happy.'

She turned to me with an outraged expression, and I at once apologized. She closed her eyes and began to speak in a low, patient voice:

'Your idea of love is rather primitive. It is not a series of sensations, independent of each other . . .'

I realized how every time I had fallen in love it had been like that: a sudden emotion, roused by a face, a gesture or a kiss, which I remember only as incoherent moments of excitement. 'It is something different,' said Anne. 'There are such things as lasting affection, sweetness, a sense of loss . . . but I suppose you wouldn't understand.'

She made an evasive gesture and took up a newspaper. If only she had been angry instead of showing that resigned indifference to my emotional irresponsibility! All the same I felt she was right: that I was governed by my instincts like an animal, swayed this way and that by other people, that I was shallow and weak. I despised myself, and it was a horribly painful sensation, all the more since I was not used to self-criticism. I went up to my room in a daze. Lying in bed on my lukewarm sheet I thought of Anne's words: 'It is something different, it's a sense of loss.' Had I ever missed anyone?

The next fortnight is rather vague in my memory because I deliberately shut my eyes to any threat to our security, but the rest of the holiday stands out all the more clearly because of the rôle I chose to play in it.

To go back to those first three weeks, three happy weeks after all: when exactly did my father begin to treat Anne with a new familiarity? Was it the day he reproached her for her indifference, while pretending to laugh at it? Or the time he grimly compared her subtlety with Elsa's semi-imbecility? My peace of mind was based on the stupid idea that they had known each other for fifteen years, and that if they had been going to fall in love, they would have done so earlier. And I thought also that if it had to happen, the affair would last at the most three months, and Anne would be left with her memories and perhaps a slight feeling of humiliation. Yet all the time I knew in my heart that Anne was not a woman who could be lightly abandoned.

But Cyril was there, and I was fully occupied. In the evenings we often drove to Saint-Tropez and danced in various bars to the soft music of a clarinet. At those moments we felt we were madly in love, but by the next morning it was all forgotten. During the day we went sailing. My father sometimes came with us. He thought a lot of Cyril, especially since he had been allowed to beat him in the swimming race. He called Cyril 'my boy', Cyril called him 'sir', but I sometimes wondered which of the two was the adult.

One afternoon we went to tea with Cyril's mother, a quiet smiling old lady who spoke to us of her difficulties as a widow and mother. My father sympathized with her, looked gratefully at Anne, and paid innumerable compliments. I must say he never minded wasting his time! Anne looked on at the spectacle with an amiable smile, and afterwards said she thought her charming. I broke into imprecations against old ladies of that sort. They both seemed amused, which made me furious.

'Don't you realize how self-righteous she is?' I insisted. 'That she pats herself on the back because she feels she has done her duty by leading a respectable bourgeois life?'

'But it is true,' said Anne. 'She has done her duty as a wife and mother, as they say.'

'You don't understand at all,' I said. 'She brought up her child; most likely she was faithful to her husband, and so had no worries; she has led the life of millions of other women, and she's proud of it. She glorifies herself for a negative reason, and not for having accomplished anything.'

'Your ideas are fashionable, but you don't know what you are talking about,' Anne said.

She was probably right: I believed what I said at the time, but I must admit that I was only repeating what I had heard. Nevertheless my life and my father's upheld that theory, and Anne hurt my feelings by despising it. One can be just as attached to futilities as to anything else. I suddenly felt an urgent desire to undeceive her. I did not think the opportunity would occur so soon, nor that I would be able to seize it. Anyhow it was quite likely that in a month's time I might have entirely different opinions on any given subject. What more could have been expected of me?

5

And then one day things came to a head. In the morning my father announced that he would like to go to Cannes that evening to dance at the casino, and perhaps gamble as well. I remember how pleased Elsa was. In the familiar casino atmosphere she hoped to resume her rôle of a 'femme fatale', slightly obscured of late by her sunburn and our semi-isolation. Contrary to my expectation Anne did not oppose our plans; she even seemed quite pleased. As soon as dinner was over I went up to my room to put on an evening frock, the only one I possessed, by the way. It had been chosen by my father, and was made of an exotic material, probably too exotic for a girl of my age, but my father, either from inclination or habit, liked to give me a veneer of sophistication. I found him downstairs, sparkling in a new dinner jacket, and I put my arms round his neck:

'You're the best-looking man I know!'

'Except Cyril,' he answered without conviction. 'And as for you, you're the prettiest girl I know.'

'After Elsa and Anne,' I replied, without believing it myself.

'Since they're not down yet, and have the cheek to keep us waiting, come and dance with your rheumaticky old father!'

Once again I felt the thrill that always preceded our evenings out together. He really had nothing of an old father about him. While dancing I inhaled the warmth of his familiar perfume, eau de cologne and tobacco. He danced slowly with half-closed eyes, a happy, irrepressible little smile, like my own, on his lips.

'You must teach me the bebop,' he said, forgetting his talk of rheumatism.

He stopped dancing to welcome Elsa with polite flattery. She came slowly down the stairs in her green dress, a conventional smile on her face, her casino smile. She had made the most of her lifeless hair and scorched skin, but the result was more meretricious than brilliant. Fortunately she seemed unaware of it.

'Are we going?'

'Anne's not here yet,' I remarked.

'Go up and see if she's ready,' said my father. 'It will be midnight before we get to Cannes.'

I ran up the stairs, getting somewhat entangled with my skirt, and knocked at Anne's door. She called to me to come in, but I stopped on the threshold. She was wearing a grey dress, a peculiar grey, almost white, which, when it caught the light, resembled the colour of the sea at dawn. She seemed to me the personification of mature charm.

'Oh Anne, what a magnificent dress!' I said.

She smiled into the mirror as one smiles at a person one is about to leave.

'This grey is a success,' she said.

'You are a success!' I answered.

She pinched my ear, her eyes were dark blue, and I saw them light up with a smile.

'You're a dear child, even though you can be tiresome at times.'

She went out in front of me without a glance at my dress. In a way I was relieved, but all the same it was mortifying. I followed her down the stairs and I saw my father coming to meet her. He stopped at the bottom, his foot on the first step, his face raised. Elsa was looking on. I remember the scene perfectly. First of all, in front of me, Anne's golden neck and perfect shoulders, a little lower down my father's fascinated face and extended hand, and, already in the distance, Elsa's silhouette.

'Anne, you are wonderful!' said my father.

She smiled as she passed him and took her coat.

'Shall we meet there?' she asked. 'Cecile, will you come with me?'

She let me drive. At night the road appeared so beautiful that I went slowly. Anne was silent; she did not even seem to notice the blaring wireless. When my father's car passed us at the bend she remained unmoved. I felt I was out of the race, watching a performance in which I could no longer intervene.

At the casino my father saw to it that we soon lost sight of each other. I found myself at the bar with Elsa and one of her acquaintances, a half-tipsy South American. He was connected with the stage and had such a passionate love for it that even in his inebriated condition he could remain amusing. I spent an agreeable hour with him, but Elsa was bored. She knew one or two big names, but that was not her world. All of a sudden she asked me where my father was, as if I had some means of knowing. She then left us. The South American seemed put out for a moment, but another whisky set him up again. My mind was a blank. I was quite light-headed, for I had been drinking with him out of politeness. It became grotesque when he wanted to dance. I was forced to hold him up and to extricate my feet from under his, which required a lot of energy. We laughed so much that when Elsa tapped me on the shoulder and I saw her Cassandra-like expression, I almost felt like telling her to go to the devil.

'I can't find them,' she said.

She looked utterly distraught. Her powder had worn off leaving her skin shiny, her features were drawn; she was a pitiable sight. I suddenly felt very angry with my father; he was being most unkind.

'Ah, I know where they are,' I said, smiling as if I referred to something quite ordinary about which she need have no anxiety. 'I'll soon be back.'

Deprived of my support, the South American fell into Elsa's arms and seemed comfortable enough there. I reflected somewhat sadly that she was more experienced than I, and that I could not very well bear her a grudge.

The casino was big, and I went all round it twice without any success. I scanned the terrace and at last thought of the car. It took me some time to find it in the car park. They were inside. I approached from behind and saw them through the rear window. Their profiles were very close together and very serious, and looked strangely beautiful in the lamplight. They were facing each other and must have been talking in low tones, for I saw their lips move. I would have liked to go away again, but the thought of Elsa made me open the door. My father had his hand on Anne's arm, and they scarcely noticed me.

'Are you having a good time?' I asked politely.

'What is the matter?' said my father irritably. 'What are you doing here?'

'And you? Elsa has been searching for you everywhere for the past hour.'

Anne turned her head slowly and reluctantly towards me.

'We're going home. Tell her I was tired and your father drove me back. When you've had enough take my car.'

I was trembling with indignation and could hardly speak:

'Had enough? But you don't realize what you're saying, it's disgusting!'

'What is disgusting?' asked my father with astonishment.

'You take a red-haired girl to the seaside, expose her to the hot sun which she can't stand, and when her skin has all peeled you abandon her. It's altogether too simple! What on earth shall I say to Elsa?'

Anne turned to him with an air of weariness. He smiled at her, obviously not listening. My exasperation knew no bounds:

'I shall tell Elsa that my father has found someone else to sleep with, and that she had better come back some other time. Is that right?'

My father's exclamation and Anne's slap were simultaneous. I hurriedly withdrew my head from the car-door. She had hurt me.

'Apologize at once!' said my father.

I stood motionless, with my thoughts in a whirl. Noble attitudes always occur to me too late.

'Come here,' said Anne.

She did not sound menacing, and I went closer. She put her hand against my cheek and spoke slowly and gently as if I were rather simple:

'Don't be naughty. I'm very sorry for Elsa, but you are tactful enough to arrange everything for the best. Tomorrow we'll discuss it. Did I hurt you very much?'

'Not at all,' I said politely. Her sudden gentleness after my intemperate rage made me want to burst into tears. I watched them drive away, feeling completely deflated. My only consolation was the thought of my tactfulness.

I walked slowly back to the casino, where I found Elsa with the South American clinging to her arm.

'Anne wasn't well,' I said in an off-hand manner. 'Papa had to take her home. What about a drink?'

She looked at me without answering, I tried to find a more convincing explanation:

'She was awfully sick,' I said. 'It was ghastly, her dress is ruined.' This detail seemed to me to make my story more plausible, but Elsa began to weep quietly and sadly. I did not know what to do.

'Oh, Cécile, we were so happy!' she said, and her sobs redoubled in intensity. The South American began to cry, repeating, 'We were so happy, so happy!' At that moment I heartily detested Anne and my father. I would have done anything to stop Elsa from crying, her eyeblack from running, and the South American from howling.

'Nothing is settled yet, Elsa. Come home with me now!'

'No! I'll fetch my suitcases later,' she sobbed. 'Goodbye, Cécile, we got on well together, didn't we?'

We had never talked of anything but clothes or the weather, but still it seemed to me that I was losing an old friend. I quickly turned away and ran to the car.

6

The following morning was wretched, probably because of the whisky I had drunk the night before. I awoke to find myself lying across my bed in the dark; my tongue heavy, my limbs unbearably damp and sticky. A single ray of sunshine filtered through the slats of the shutters and I could see a million motes dancing in it. I felt no desire to get up, nor to stay in bed. I wondered how Anne and my father would look if Elsa were to turn up that morning. I forced myself to think of them in order to be able to get out of bed without effort. At last I managed to stand up on the cool stone floor. I was giddy and aching. The mirror reflected a sad sight; I leant against it and peered at those dilated eyes and dry lips, an unknown face; mine? If I was weak and cowardly, could it be because of those lips, the particular shape of my body, these odious, arbitrary limits? And if I were limited, why had I only now become aware of it? I amused myself by detesting my reflection, hating that wolf-like face, hollow and worn by debauch. I repeated the word 'debauch' dumbly, looking into my eyes in the mirror, and suddenly I saw myself smile. What a debauch! A few unfortunate drinks, a slap in the face and some tears! I brushed my teeth and went downstairs.

My father and Anne were already on the terrace sitting beside each other in front of their breakfast tray. I sat down opposite them, muttering a vague 'good morning'. A feeling of shyness made me keep my eyes lowered, but after a time, as they remained silent I was forced to look at them. Anne appeared tired, the only sign of a night of love. They were both smiling happily, and I was very much impressed, for happiness has always seemed to me a great achievement.

'Did you sleep well?' asked my father.

'Not too badly,' I replied. 'I drank a lot of whisky last night.'

I poured out a cup of coffee, but after the first sip I quickly put it down. Their silence had a waiting quality that made me feel uneasy. I was too tired to bear it for long.

'What's the matter? You look so mysterious.'

My father lit a cigarette, making an obvious effort to seem unconcerned, and for once in her life Anne seemed embarrassed.

'I would like to ask you something,' she said at last.

'I suppose you want me to take another message to Elsa?' I said, imagining the worst.

She turned towards my father:

'Your father and I want to get married,' she said.

I stared first at her, then at my father. I half expected some sign from him, perhaps a wink, which, though I might have found it shocking, would have reassured me, but he was looking down at his hands. I said to myself 'it can't be possible!', but I already knew it was true.

'What a good idea!' I said to gain time.

I could not understand how my father, who had always set himself so obstinately against marriage and its chains, could have decided on it in a single night. We were about to lose our independence. I could visualize our future family life, a life which would suddenly be given equilibrium by Anne's intelligence and refinement; the life I had envied her. We would have clever tactful friends, and quiet pleasant evenings . . . I found myself despising noisy dinners, South Americans and girls like Elsa. I felt proud and superior.

'It's a very, very good idea,' I repeated, and I smiled at them.

'I knew you'd be pleased, my pet,' said my father.

He was relaxed and delighted. Anne's face, subtly changed by love, seemed gentler, making her appear more accessible than she had ever been before.

'Come here, my pet,' said my father; and holding out his hands, he drew me close to them both. I was half-kneeling in front of them, while they stroked my hair and looked at me with tender emotion. But I could not stop thinking that although my life was perhaps at that very moment changing its whole course, I was in reality nothing more than a kitten to them, an affectionate little animal. I felt them above me, united by a past and a future, by ties that I did not know and which could not hold me. But I deliberately closed my eyes and went on playing my part, laying my head on their knees and laughing. For was I not happy? Anne was all right, I had no serious fault to find with her. She would guide me, relieve me of responsibility, and be at hand whenever I might need her. She would make both my father and me into paragons of virtue.

My father got up to fetch a bottle of champagne. I felt sickened. He was happy, which was the chief thing, but I had so often seen him happy on account of a woman.

'I was rather frightened of you,' said Anne.

'Why?' I asked. Her words had given me the impression that a veto from me could have prevented their marriage.

'I was afraid of your being frightened of me,' she said laughing.

I began to laugh too, because actually I was a little scared of her. She wanted me to understand that she knew it, and that it was unnecessary.

'Does the marriage of two people like ourselves seem ridiculous to you?'

'You're not old,' I said emphatically, as my father came dancing back with a bottle in his hand.

He sat down next to Anne and put his arm round her shoulders. She moved nearer to him and I looked away in embarrassment. She was no doubt marrying him for just that; for his laughter, for the firm reassurance of his arm, for his vitality, his warmth. At forty there could be the fear of solitude, or perhaps a last upsurge of the senses . . . I had never thought of Anne as a woman, but as an entity. I had seen her as a self-assured, elegant, and clever person, but never weak or sensual. I quite understood that my father felt proud, the self-satisfied, indifferent Anne Larsen was going to marry him. Did he love her, and if so, was he capable of loving her for long? Was there any difference between this new feeling and the affection he had shown Elsa? The sun was making my head spin, and I shut my eyes. We were all three on the terrace, full of reserves, of secret fears, and of happiness.

Elsa did not come back just then. A week flew by, seven happy, agreeable days, the only ones. We made elaborate plans for furnishing our home, and discussed timetables which my father and I took pleasure in cutting as fine as possible with the blind obstinacy of those who have never had any use for them. Did we ever believe in them for one moment? Did my father really think it possible to have lunch every day at the same place at 12.30 sharp, to have dinner at home, and not to go out afterwards? However, he gaily prepared to inter Bohemianism, and began to preach order, and to extol the joys of an elegant, organized bourgeois existence. No doubt for him, as well as for myself, all these plans were merely castles in the air.

How well I remember that week! Anne was relaxed, confident, and very sweet; my father loved her. I saw them coming down in the mornings, leaning on each other, laughing gaily, with shadows under their eyes, and I swear that I should have liked nothing better than that their happiness should last all their lives. In the evening we often drank our apéritif sitting on some café terrace by the sea. Everywhere we went we were taken for a happy, normal family, and I, who was used to going out alone with my father and seeing the knowing smiles, and malicious or pitying glances, was delighted to play a rôle more suitable to my age. They were to be married on our return to Paris.

Poor Cyril had witnessed the transformation in our midst with a certain amazement, but he was comforted by the thought that this time it would be legalized. We went out sailing together and kissed when we felt inclined, but sometimes during our embraces I thought of Anne's face as I saw it in the mornings, with its softened contours. I recalled the happy nonchalance, the languid grace that love imparted to her movements, and I envied her. One can grow tired of kissing, and no doubt if Cyril had not been so fond of me I would have become his mistress that week.

At six o'clock, on our return from the islands, Cyril would pull the boat into the sand. We would go up to the house through the pine wood in single file, pretending we were Indians, or run handicap races to warm ourselves up. He always caught me before we reached the house and would spring on me with a shout of victory, rolling me on the pine needles, pinning my arms down and kissing me. I can still remember those light, breathless kisses, and Cyril's heart beating against mine in rhythm with the soft thud of the waves on the sand. Four heart-beats and four waves, and then gradually he would regain his breath and his kisses would become more urgent, the sound of the sea would grow dim and give way to the pulse in my ears.

One evening we were surprised by Anne's voice. Cyril was lying close to me in the red glow of the sunset. I can understand that Anne might have been misled by the sight of us there in our scanty bathing things. She called me sharply.

Cyril bounded to his feet, naturally somewhat ashamed. Keeping my eyes on Anne, I slowly got up in my turn. She faced Cyril, and looking right through him spoke in a quiet voice: 'I don't wish to see you again.'

He made no reply, but bent over and kissed my shoulder before departing. I felt surprised and touched, as if his gesture had been a sort of pledge. Anne was staring at me with the same grave and detached look, as though she were thinking of something else. Her manner infuriated me. If she was so deep in thought, why speak at all? I went up to her, feigning embarrassment for the sake of politeness. At last she seemed to notice me and mechanically removed a pine needle from my neck. I saw her face assume its beautiful mask of disdain, that expression of weariness and disapproval which became her so well, and which always frightened me a little.

'You should know that such diversions usually end up in a nursing home.'

She stood there looking straight at me as she spoke, and I was horribly ashamed. She was one of those women who can stand perfectly still while they talk; I always needed the support of a chair, or some object to hold like a cigarette, or the distraction of swinging one leg over the other and watching it move.

'You mustn't exaggerate,' I said with a smile. 'I was only kissing Cyril, and that won't lead me to any nursing home.'

'Please don't see him again,' she said, as if she did not believe me. 'Do not protest: you are seventeen and I feel a certain responsibility for you now. I'm not going to let you ruin your life. In any case you have work to do, and that will occupy your afternoons.'

She turned her back on me and walked towards the house in her nonchalant way. A paralysing sense of calamity kept me rooted to the spot. She had meant every word; what was the use of arguments or denials when she would receive them with the sort of indifference that was worse than contempt, as if I did not even exist, as if I were something to be squashed underfoot, and not myself, Cécile, whom she had always known. My only hope now was my father; surely he would say as usual: 'Well now, who's the boy? I suppose he's a handsome fellow, but beware, my girl!' If he did not react like this, my holidays would be ruined.

Dinner was a nightmare. Not for one moment had Anne suggested that she would not tell my father anything if I promised to work; it was not in her nature to bargain. I was pleased in one way, but also disappointed that she had deprived me of a chance to despise her. As usual she avoided a false move, and it was only when we had finished our soup that she seemed to remember the incident.

'I do wish you'd give your daughter some advice, Raymond. I found her in the wood with Cyril this evening, and they seemed to be going rather far.'

My father, poor man, tried to pass the whole thing off as a joke.

'What's that you say? What were they up to?'

'I was kissing him,' I said. 'And Anne thought . . .'

'I never thought anything at all,' she interrupted. 'But it might be a good idea for her to stop seeing him for a time and to work at her philosophy instead.'

'Poor little thing!' said my father. 'After all Cyril's a nice boy, isn't he?'

'And Cécile is a nice girl,' said Anne. 'That's why I should be heartbroken if anything should happen to her, and it seems to me inevitable that it will, if you consider what complete freedom she enjoys here, and that they are constantly together and have nothing whatever to do. Don't you agree?'

At her last words I looked up and saw that my father was very perturbed.

'You are probably right,' he said. 'After all, you ought to do some work, Cécile. You surely don't want to fail in philosophy and have to take it again?'

'What do you think I care?' I answered.

He glanced at me and then turned away. I was bewildered. I

realized that procrastination can rule our lives, yet not provide us with any arguments in its defence.

'Listen,' said Anne, taking my hand across the table. 'Won't you exchange your rôle of a wood nymph for that of a good schoolgirl for one month? Would it be so serious?'

They both looked at me expectantly; seen in that light, the argument was simple enough. I gently withdrew my hand.

'Yes, very serious,' I said, so softly that they did not hear it, or did not want to.

The following morning I came across a phrase from Bergson:

Whatever irrelevance one may at first find between the cause and the effects, and although a rule of guidance towards an assertion concerning the root of things may be far distant, it is always in a contact with the generative force of life that one is able to extract the power to love humanity.

I repeated the phrase, quietly at first, so as not to get agitated, then in a louder voice. I held my head in my hands and looked at the book with great attention. At last I understood it, but I felt as cold and impotent as when I had read it the first time. I could not continue. With the best will in the world I applied myself to the next lines, and suddenly something arose in me like a storm and threw me on to the bed. I thought of Cyril waiting for me down in the creek, of the swaying boat, of the pleasure of our kisses, and then I thought of Anne, but in a way that made me sit up on my bed with a fast-beating heart, telling myself that I was stupid, monstrous, nothing but a lazy, spoilt child, and had no right to have such thoughts. But all the same, in spite of myself I continued to reflect that she was dangerous, and that I must get rid of her. I thought of the lunch I had endured with clenched teeth, tortured by a feeling of resentment for which I despised and ridiculed myself. Yes, it was for this I reproached Anne: she prevented me from liking myself. I, who was so naturally meant for happiness and gaiety, had been forced by her into a world of self-criticism and guilty conscience, where, unaccustomed to intro-spection, I was completely lost. And what did she bring me? I took stock: She wanted my father; she had got him. She would gradu-ally make of us the husband and step-daughter of Anne Larsen; that is to say, she would turn us into two civilized, well-behaved and happy people. For she would certainly make us happy. How easily, unstable and irresponsible as we were, we would yield to her influence, and be drawn into the attractive framework of her orderly plan of living. She was much too efficient: already my father was estranged from me. I was obsessed by his embarrassed face turning away from me at table. Tears came into my eyes at the thought of the jokes we used to have together, our laughter as we drove home at dawn through the empty streets of Paris. All that was over. In my turn I would be influenced, re-orientated, re-modelled by Anne. I would not even mind it, she would act with intelligence, irony and sweetness, and I would be incapable of resistance; in six months I should no longer even wish to resist.

At all costs I must take steps to regain my father and our former life. How infinitely desirable those two years suddenly appeared to me, those happy years I was so willing to renounce the other day . . . the liberty to think, even to think wrongly or not at all, the freedom to choose my own life, to choose myself. I cannot say 'to be myself', for I was only soft clay, but still I could refuse to be moulded.

I realize that one might find complicated motives for this change in me, one might endow me with spectacular complexes: such as an incestuous love for my father, or a morbid passion for Anne, but I know the true reasons were the heat, Bergson, and Cyril, or at least his absence. I dwelt on this all the afternoon in a most unpleasant mood, induced by the discovery that we were entirely at Anne's mercy. I was not used to reflection, and it made me irritable. At dinner, as in the morning, I did not open my mouth. My father thought it appropriate to chaff me:

'What I like about youth is its spontaneity, its gay conversation.'

I was trembling with rage. It was true that he loved youth; and with whom could I have talked if not with him? We had discussed everything together: love, death, music. Now he himself had disarmed and abandoned me. Looking at him I thought: 'You don't love me any more, you have betrayed me!' I tried to make him understand without words how desperate I was. He seemed suddenly alarmed; perhaps he understood that the time for joking was past, and that our relationship was in danger. I saw him stiffen, and it appeared as though he were about to ask a question. Anne turned to me:

'You don't look well. I feel sorry now for making you work.'

I did not reply. I felt too disgusted that I had got myself into a state which I could no longer control. We had finished dinner. On the terrace, in the rectangle of light projected from the dining-room window, I saw Anne's long nervous hand reach out to find my father's. I thought of Cyril. I would have liked him to take me in his arms on that moonlight terrace, alive with crickets. I would have liked to be caressed, consoled, reconciled with myself. My father and Anne were silent, they had a night of love to look forward to; I had Bergson. I tried to cry, to feel sorry for myself, but in vain; it was already Anne for whom I was sorry, as if I were certain of victory.

PART TWO

I

I am surprised how clearly I remember everything from that moment. I acquired an added awareness of other people and of myself. Until then I had always been spontaneous and light-hearted, but the last few days had upset me to the extent of forcing me to reflect and to look at myself with a critical eye. However, I seemed to come no nearer to a solution of my problems. I kept telling myself that my feelings about Anne were mean and stupid, and that my desire to separate her from my father was vicious. Then I would argue that after all I had every right to feel as I did. For the first time in my life I was divided against myself. Up in my room I reasoned with myself for hours on end in an attempt to discover whether the fear and hostility which Anne inspired in me were justified, or if I were merely a silly, spoilt, selfish girl in a mood of sham independence.

In the meantime I grew thinner every day. On the beach I did nothing but sleep, and at meal-times I maintained a strained silence that ended by making the others feel uneasy. And all the time I watched Anne. At dinner I would say to myself, 'Doesn't every movement she makes prove how much she loves him? Could anyone be more in love? How can I be angry with her when she smiles at me with that trace of anxiety in her eyes?' But suddenly she would say, 'When we get home, Raymond . . .' and the thought that she was going to share our life and interfere with us would arouse me again. Once more she seemed calculating and cold. I thought: 'She is cold, we are warm-hearted, she is possessive, we are independent. She is indifferent; other people don't interest her, we love them. She is reserved, we are gay. We are full of life and she will slink in between us with her sobriety; she will warm herself at our fire and gradually rob us of our enthusiasm; like a beautiful serpent she will rob us of everything.' I repeated 'a beautiful serpent' . . . she passed me the bread, and suddenly I came to my senses. 'But it's crazy,' I thought. 'That's Anne, your friend who was so kind to you, who is so clever. Her aloofness is a mere outward form, there's nothing calculated about it, her indifference shields her from the countless sordid things in life, it's a sign of nobility.' A beautiful serpent . . . I felt myself turn pale with shame. I looked at her, silently imploring her forgiveness. At times she noticed my expression and a shadow of surprise and uncertainty clouded her face and made her break off in the middle of a sentence. Her eyes turned instinctively to my father; but his glance held nothing but admiration or desire, he did not understand the cause of her disquiet. Little by little I made the atmosphere unbearable, and I detested myself for it.

My father suffered as much as his nature permitted, that is to say hardly at all, for he was mad about Anne, madly proud and happy, and nothing else existed for him. However, one day when I was dozing on the beach after my morning bathe, he sat down next to me and looked at me closely. I felt his eyes upon me, and with the air of false gaiety that was fast becoming a habit I was just going to ask him to come in for a swim when he put his hand on my head and called to Anne in a doleful voice:

'Come over here and have a look at this creature; she's as thin as a rake. If this is the effect work has on her, she'll have to give it up!'

He thought that would settle everything, and no doubt it would have done so ten days earlier. But now I was too deeply immersed in complications, and the hours set aside for work in the afternoons no longer bothered me, especially as I had not opened a book since Bergson.

Anne came up to us. I remained lying face down on the sand listening to the muffled sound of her footsteps. She sat on my other side.

'It certainly doesn't seem to agree with her,' she said. 'But if she really did work instead of walking up and down in her room . . .'

I had turned round and was looking at them. How did she know that I was not working? Perhaps she had even read my thoughts? I believed her to be capable of anything.

I protested:

'I don't walk up and down in my room!'

'Do you miss that boy?' asked my father.

'No!'

This was not quite true, but I certainly had had no time to think of Cyril.

'But still, you're not well,' said my father firmly. 'Anne, do you notice it too? She looks like a chicken that has been drawn and then put to roast in the sun.'

'Make an effort, Cécile dear,' said Anne. 'Do a little work and try to eat a lot. That exam is important . . .'

'I don't care a hang about the exam!' I cried. 'Can't you understand? I just don't care!'

I looked straight at her, despairingly, so that she should realize that something more serious than my examination was at stake. I longed for her to ask me: 'Well, what is it?' and ply me with questions, and force me to tell her everything: then I would be won over and she could do anything she liked with me, and I should no longer be in torment. She looked at me attentively. I could see the Prussian blue of her eyes darken with concentration and reproach. Then I understood that it would never occur to her to question me and so deliver me from myself, because even if the thought had entered her head, her code of behaviour would have precluded it. And I saw too that she had no idea of the tumult within me, or even if she had, her attitude would have been one of indifference and disdain, which was in any case what I deserved! Anne always gave everything its exact value, that is why I could never come to an understanding with her.

I dropped back on to the sand and laid my cheek against its soft warmth. I sighed deeply and began to tremble. I could feel Anne's hand, tranquil and steady, on the back of my neck, holding me still for a moment, just long enough to stop my nervous tremor.

'Don't complicate life for yourself,' she said. 'You've always been so contented and lively, and had no head for anything serious. It doesn't suit you to be pensive and sad.'

'I know that,' I answered. 'I'm just a thoughtless healthy young thing, brimful of gaiety and stupidity!'

'Come and have lunch,' she said.

My father had moved away from us; he detested that sort of discussion. On the way back he took my hand and held it. His hand was firm and comforting: it had dried my tears after my first disappointment in love, it had closed over mine in moments of tranquillity and perfect happiness, it had stealthily pressed mine at times of complicity or riotous laughter. I thought of his hand on the steering wheel, or holding the keys at night and searching in vain for the lock; his hand on a woman's shoulder, or holding a cigarette, the hand that could do nothing more for me. I gave it a hard squeeze. Turning towards me, he smiled.

2

Two days went by: I went round in circles, I wore myself out, but I could not free myself from the haunting thought that Anne was about to wreck our lives. I did not try to see Cyril; he would have comforted me and made me happier, but that was not what I wanted. I even got a certain satisfaction from asking myself insoluble questions, by reminding myself of days gone by, and dreading those to come. It was very hot; my room was in semi-darkness with the shutters closed, but even so the air was unbearably heavy and damp. I lay on my bed staring at the ceiling, hardly moving except to search for a cool place on the sheet. I did not sleep, but played records on the gramophone at the foot of my bed. I chose slow rhythms, without any tune. I smoked a good deal and felt decadent, which gave me pleasure. But I was not deluded by this game of pretence: I was sad and bewildered.

One afternoon the maid knocked at my door and announced with an air of mystery: 'Someone's downstairs.' I at once thought of Cyril and went down. It was not Cyril, but Elsa. She greeted me effusively. Looking at her, I was astonished at her new beauty. She was tanned at last, evenly and smoothly, and was carefully made up and brilliantly youthful.

'I've come to fetch my suitcase,' she explained. 'Juan bought me a few dresses, but not enough, and I need my things.'

I wondered for a moment who Juan could be, but did not enquire further. I was pleased Elsa had come back. She brought with her the aura of a kept woman, of bars, of gay evenings, which reminded me of happier days. I told her how glad I was to see her again, and she assured me that we had always got on so well together because we had common interests. I suppressed a slight shudder and suggested that we should go up to my room to avoid meeting Anne and my father. When I mentioned my father she made an involuntary movement with her head, and I wondered whether perhaps she was still in love with him, in spite of Juan and the dresses. I also thought that three weeks before I would not have noticed that movement of hers.

In my room I listened while she described in glowing terms her smart and dizzy life in the fashionable places along the Riviera. A strange confusion of thoughts went through my head, partly suggested by her different appearance. At last she stopped talking, perhaps because I was silent. She took a few steps across the room, and without turning round asked in an off-hand way if Raymond was happy. In a moment I knew what I must say to her:

'"Happy" is saying too much! Anne doesn't give him a chance to think otherwise. She is very clever.'

'Very!' sighed Elsa.

'You'll never guess what she's persuaded him to do . . . she's going to marry him . . .'

Elsa turned a horrified face towards me:

'Marry him? Raymond actually wants to get married?'

'Yes,' I answered. 'Raymond is going to be married.'

A sudden desire to laugh caught me by the throat. My hands were shaking. Elsa seemed prostrated, almost as if I had given her a knockout blow. On no account must she be allowed to realize that after all he was of an age to marry, and could not be expected to spend his life with women of her sort. I leant forward and suddenly lowered my voice to make a stronger impression on her:

'It simply mustn't happen, Elsa. He's suffering already. It's an impossible state of affairs, as you can very well imagine.'

'Yes,' she said.

She seemed fascinated.

'You're just the person I've been waiting for,' I went on, 'because you are the only one who is a match for Anne. You alone are up to her standard.'

She seemed to swallow the bait.

'But if he's marrying her it must be because he loves her?' she objected.

'But look here, Elsa, it's you he loves! Do you want to make me believe that you don't know it?'

I saw her bat her eyelids, and she turned away to hide her pleasure, and the hope my words had given her. I was prompted by a sort of infallible instinct and I knew just how to continue.

'Don't you see? Anne kept harping on the bliss of married life, morality, and all that, and in the end she caught him.'

I was surprised at my own words. For even though I had expressed myself somewhat crudely, that was just what I felt.

'If they get married, our lives will be ruined, Elsa! My father must be protected, he's nothing but a big baby . . .'

I repeated 'a big baby' with stronger emphasis. It seemed to me that I was being rather too melodramatic, but I saw Elsa's beautiful green eyes fill with pity, and I ended up, like in a canticle:

'Help me, Elsa! It's for your own sake, for my father, and for the love between you.'

I added to myself: 'and for Johnny Chinaman!'

'But what can I do?' asked Elsa. 'It seems an impossible situation.'

'If you think it's impossible, then give up the idea,' I said sadly.

'What a bitch!' murmured Elsa.

'You've hit the nail on the head,' I said, turning away to hide my expression.

Elsa visibly brightened up. She had been jilted, and now she was going to show that adventuress just what she, Elsa Mackenbourg, could do. And my father loved her, as she had always known he did. Even while she had been with Juan she hadn't been able to put Raymond out of her mind. She'd never as much as mentioned the word marriage to him, and she had never bored him either, and she'd never tried . . . but by now I could endure her no longer:

'Elsa,' I said, 'go and ask Cyril from me if you could possibly stay with his mother; say you are in need of hospitality. Tomorrow morning I'll come and see him, and we'll all three discuss the situation.'

On the doorstep I added for a joke: 'You are fighting for your own future, Elsa!'

She gravely acquiesced as if there were not fifteen or twenty 'futures' in store for her, in the shape of men who would keep her. I watched her walking away in the sunshine with her mincing steps. I thought it would not be a week before my father wanted her back.

It was half past three; I imagined my father asleep in Anne's arms. I began to formulate plans one after another without pausing to think of myself. I walked up and down in my room between the door and the window, looking out from time to time at the calm sea flattening out along the beach. I calculated risks, estimated possibilities, and gradually I broke down every objection. I felt dangerously clever, and the wave of self-disgust which had swept over me from the moment I had begun to talk to Elsa now gave place to a feeling of pride in my own capabilities.

I need hardly say that all this collapsed when we went down to bathe. As soon as I saw Anne, I was overcome by remorse and did my utmost to atone for my past behaviour. I carried her bag, I rushed forward with her wrap when she came out of the water. I smothered her with attention and said the nicest things. This sudden change after my silence of the past few days was naturally a surprise to her. My father was delighted, Anne smiled at me. I thought of the words I had used in speaking of her to Elsa. How could I have said them, and how could I have put up with Elsa's nonsense? Tomorrow I would advise her to go away, saying that I had made a mistake. Everything would be as before, and, after all, why should I not pass my examination? The *baccalauréat* was sure to come in useful.

'Isn't that so?' I asked Anne. 'Isn't it useful to get one's *baccalauréat*?'

She gave me a look and burst out laughing. I followed suit, happy to see her so gay.

'You're really incredible!' she exclaimed.

I certainly was incredible, and she would have thought me even more so if she had known what I had been planning. I was dying to tell her all about it so that she could see how incredible I could be. I would have said: 'Can you imagine that I was going to make Elsa pretend to be in love with Cyril; she was to go and stay in his house, and we would have seen them passing by on his boat; strolling in the wood or along the road. Elsa looks lovely again; of course she hasn't your beauty, hers is the flamboyant kind that makes men turn round. My father wouldn't have stood it for long, he has never tolerated that a good-looking woman who had lived with him should console herself so soon, and, so to speak, before his very eyes, and above all with a man younger than himself. You understand, Anne, he would have wanted her again very quickly even though he loves you, just in order to bolster up his morale. He's very vain, or not very sure of himself, whichever way you like to put it. Elsa, under my direction, would have done all that was necessary. One day he would have been unfaithful to you and you couldn't bear that, could you? You're not one of those women who can share a man. So you would have gone away and that was exactly what I wanted. It's stupid, I know, but I was angry with you because of Bergson, of the heat; I somehow imagined . . . I daren't even tell you, it was so ridiculous and unreal. On account of my *baccalauréat* I might have quarrelled with you for ever. But it's useful to have one's *baccalauréat* all the same, isn't it . . .' 'Isn't it?' I said aloud.

'What are you trying to say?' asked Anne. 'That the *baccalauréat* is useful?'

'Yes,' I replied.

After all it was better not to tell her anything, perhaps she would not have understood. There were things Anne did not understand at all. I ran into the sea after my father and wrestled with him. Once more I was able to enjoy frolicking in the water, for I had a good conscience. Tomorrow I would change my room; I would move up to the attic with my lesson books, but Bergson would not be among them; there was no need to overdo it! For two hours every day I would concentrate in solitude on my work. I imagined myself being successful in October, and thought of my father's astonished laugh, Anne's approbation, my degree. I would be intelligent, cultured, some-what aloof, like Anne. Perhaps I had intellectual gifts? Hadn't I been capable of producing a logical plan, despicable perhaps, but logical? And what about Elsa? I had known how to appeal to her vanity and sentimentality, and within a few minutes had managed to persuade her, when her only object in coming had been to fetch a suitcase. I felt proud of myself: I had taken stock of Elsa, found her weak spot, and carefully aimed my words. For the first time in my life I had known the intense pleasure of getting under another person's skin. It was a new experience; in the past I had always been too impulsive, and whenever I had come close to someone, it had been inadvertently. Now, when I had caught a sudden glimpse of the marvellous mechanism of human reflexes, and the power of speech, I felt sorry that I had come to it through lies. The day might come when I would love someone passionately, and would have to search warily and gently for the way to him.

3

Walking down to Cyril's villa the next morning, I felt far less sure of myself. To celebrate my recovery I had drunk too much at dinner the night before, and had been rather more than gay. I had told my father that I was going to take my degree, and would associate in future only with highbrows; that I wanted to become famous and a thorough bore. I said he must make use of every scandalous trick known to publicity in order to launch me. Roaring with laughter, we exchanged the most far-fetched ideas. Anne laughed too, but indulgently and not so loudly. When I became too extravagant, she stopped laughing altogether, but our hilarious fun had put my father into such a happy frame of mind that she said nothing. At last they went to bed, after tucking me up. I thanked them from the bottom of my heart, and asked what I would do without them. My father had no answer, but Anne seemed to have very decided views on the subject. Just as she leaned over to speak to me, I fell asleep. In the middle of the night I was sick, and my awakening the next morning was the worst I could ever remember. Still feeling very muzzy and in low spirits, I walked slowly towards the wood, but had no eyes for the sea, or for the skimming swallows.

Cyril was at the garden gate. He rushed towards me, took me in his arms, and held me tightly, talking incoherently:

'I was so worried, Darling . . . it's been so long . . . I had no idea what you were doing, or if that woman was making you unhappy ... I've never been so miserable ... Several times I spent all the afternoon near your creek ... I didn't know I loved you so much ...'

'Neither did I.'

To tell the truth, I was both surprised and touched, but I could hardly express my emotion because I felt so sick.

'How pale you are,' he said. 'From now on I'm going to look after you. I won't let you be ill-treated any more.'

I recognized Elsa's exaggerations, and asked Cyril what his mother thought of her.

'I introduced her as a friend of yours, an orphan. As a matter of fact she's very nice, she told me all about that woman. How strange it seems that, with a face like hers, she should be such an adventuress.'

'Elsa is too sensational,' I said weakly. 'But I was going to tell her ...'

'I too, have something to tell you,' interrupted Cyril. 'Cécile, I want to marry you.'

I had a moment of panic. I absolutely had to do or say something. If only I had not felt so ill!

'I love you,' said Cyril, speaking into my hair. 'I'll give up studying law, an uncle has offered me an interesting job. I'm twenty-six. I'm not a boy any longer; I am quite serious. What do you say?'

I tried desperately to think of a non-committal, a high-sounding phrase. I did not want to marry him. I loved him, but marriage was out of the question. I had no intention of marrying anyone. I was tired.

'It's quite impossible,' I stammered. 'My father ...'

'I'll manage your father,' said Cyril.

'Anne wouldn't approve,' I said. 'She doesn't think I'm grown-up. If she says no, my father will say the same. I'm exhausted, Cyril. All this emotion wears me out. Here's Elsa!'

She was wearing a dressing-gown, and looked fresh and radiant. I felt dull and thin. They both seemed to be overflowing with health and high spirits, which depressed me even more. She treated me as though I had come out of prison, and fussed over me, while I sat down.

'How is Raymond?' she asked. 'Does he know that I'm back?'

She had the happy smile of one who has forgiven and is full of hope. How could I tell her that my father had forgotten her, and explain to Cyril that I did not want to marry him? I shut my eyes. Cyril went to fetch some coffee. Elsa talked on and on. She obviously thought me a very subtle person in whom she could have confidence. The coffee was strong and aromatic, the sun was hot; I began to feel a little better.

'I've thought and thought, but without finding a solution,' said Elsa.

'There isn't one,' said Cyril. 'It's an infatuation; there's nothing to be done.'

'Oh yes there is!' I said. 'You just haven't any imagination.'

It flattered me to see how they hung on my words. They were ten years older than I, and they had no ideas. I said with a superior air:

'It is a question of psychology.'

I went on to explain my plan. They raised the same objections as I had done myself the day before, and I felt a particular pleasure in refuting them. I got excited all over again, in my effort to convince them that it was feasible. It only remained for me to prove to them that it ought not to be carried out, but for this I could not find any logical argument.

'I don't like that kind of intrigue,' said Cyril reluctantly. 'But if it is the only way to make you marry me, I'll do it.'

'It's not exactly Anne's fault,' I said.

'You know very well that if she stays you'll have to marry the man she chooses,' said Elsa.

Perhaps it was true. I could see Anne introducing me on my twentieth birthday to a young man with a degree to match my own, assured of a brilliant future, steady and faithful. In fact someone like Cyril himself. I began to laugh.

'Please don't laugh,' said Cyril. 'Tell me that you'll be jealous when I'm pretending to be in love with Elsa. How can you bear the thought of it for one moment? Do you love me?'

He spoke in a low voice. Elsa had gone off and discreetly left us alone. I looked at Cyril's tense brown face, his dark eyes. It gave me a strange feeling to think he loved me. I looked at his red lips, so near mine. I did not feel intellectual any longer. He came closer, our lips met and he kissed me passionately. I realized that I was more gifted for kissing a young man in the sunshine than for taking a degree. I grew away from him, gasping for breath.

'Cécile, let's stay together for ever! In the meantime I'll carry out the plan with Elsa.'

I wondered if I was right in my reckoning. As I was the instigator of the whole thing I could always stop it.

'You're full of ideas,' said Cyril with his slanting smile that lifted one side of his mouth and gave him the appearance of a handsome bandit.

And that is how I set the whole comedy in motion, against my better judgement. Sometimes I think I would blame myself less if I had been prompted that day by hatred and violence, and had not allowed myself to drift into it merely through inertia, the sun, and Cyril's kisses.

When I left the conspirators at the end of an hour, I was rather perturbed. However, there were still grounds for reassurance: my plan could misfire because my father's passion for Anne might well keep him faithful to her, besides which, neither Cyril nor Elsa could do much without my connivance. If my father showed any signs of falling into the trap, I would find some means of putting an end to the whole thing. But still it was amusing to try the plan out, and see whether my psychological judgement proved right or wrong.

What is more, Cyril was in love with me and had asked me to marry him. This was enough to make me forget everything else. If he could wait two years, to give me time to grow up, I would accept him. I could already imagine myself living with Cyril, sleeping next to him, never leaving him. Every Sunday we would go to lunch with Anne and my father, a united married couple, and sometimes perhaps include Cyril's mother, which would add a homely atmosphere to the meal.

I met Anne on the terrace on her way down to the beach to join my father. She received me with the ironical smile with which one greets those who have drunk too much the night before. I asked her what she had been going to tell me just as I fell asleep, but she only laughed and said it might make me cross. Just then my father came out of the water. He was broad and muscular, and I thought he looked wonderful. I bathed with Anne, who swam slowly with her head well out of the water so as not to wet her hair. Afterwards we three lay side by side on our stomachs in the sand, with me in the middle. We were quiet and peaceful.

Just then the boat appeared round the rocks, all sails set. My father was the first to see it.

'So Cyril couldn't hold out any longer!' he said laughing. 'Shall we forgive him, Anne? After all he's a nice boy.'

I raised my head, scenting danger.

'But what is he up to?' said my father. 'He's not coming in after all. Ah! He's not alone.'

Anne had also turned to look. The boat was going to pass right in front of us before tacking. I could make out Cyril's face. Silently I prayed that he would go away, but I could already hear my father's exclamation of surprise:

'But it's Elsa! What on earth is she doing there?'

He turned to Anne: 'That girl is extraordinary! She must already have got her claws into that poor boy and made the old lady accept her.'

But Anne was not listening; she was watching me. I saw her and hid my face in the sand to cover my shame. She put out her hand and touched my neck:

'Look at me. Are you angry with me?'

I opened my eyes. She bent over me anxiously and almost imploringly. For the first time she was treating me as a sensible, thinking person, and just on the day when ... I groaned and jerked my head round towards my father to free myself from that hand. He was watching the boat.

'My poor child,' Anne was saying in a low voice. 'Poor little Cécile! I'm afraid it is all my fault. Perhaps I shouldn't have been so hard on you. I never wanted to hurt you, do you believe me?'

She gently stroked my hair and neck. I kept quite still. I had the same feeling as when a receding wave dragged the sand away beneath me. Neither anger nor desire had ever worked so strongly in me as my longing at that moment for utter defeat. My one wish was to give up all my plans and put myself entirely into her hands for the rest of my life. I had never before been so overcome with a sense of my utter impotence. I closed my eyes. It seemed to me that my heart stopped beating.

4

So far my father had shown no feeling other than surprise. The maid told him that Elsa had been to fetch her suitcase, but said nothing about our conversation. Being a peasant woman with a romantic turn of mind, she must have relished the various changes that had taken place in our household since she had been with us, especially in the bedrooms.

My father and Anne, in their effort to make amends, were so kind to me that at first I found it unbearable. However I soon changed my mind, for even though I had brought it on myself, I did not find it very agreeable to see Cyril and Elsa walking about arm-in-arm, showing every sign of pleasure in each other's company. I could no longer go sailing myself, but I could watch Elsa as she passed by; her hair blown by the wind, as mine used to be. It was easy enough for me to look unconcerned when we met, as we did at every corner: in the wood, in the village, and on the road. Anne would glance at me, start a new topic of conversation, and put her hand on my shoulder to comfort me. Have I ever mentioned how kind she was? Whether her kindness emanated from her intelligence, or was merely part of her detachment, I do not know, but she had an unerring instinct for the right word, and if I had really been unhappy, I could hardly have found better support.

As my father gave no signs of jealousy, I was not unduly worried, and allowed things to drift; but while it proved to me how fond he was of Anne, I felt rather annoyed that my plan had misfired. One day he and I were on our way to the post office when we passed Elsa. She pretended not to see us, and my father turned round after her with a whistle of surprise, as if she had been a stranger:

'I say! Hasn't she become a beauty!'

'Love seems to agree with her,' I remarked.

He looked rather astonished: 'You're taking it very well, I must say!'

'What can one do? They're the same age. I suppose it was inevitable.'

'If Anne hadn't come along, it wouldn't have been inevitable at all!' he said angrily. 'You don't think I'd let a boy like that snatch a woman from me without my consent?'

'All the same, age tells!' I said solemnly.

He shrugged his shoulders. On the way back I noticed he was preoccupied: perhaps he was thinking that both Cyril and Elsa were young, and that in marrying a woman of his own age, he would cease to belong to the category of men whose age does not count. I had a momentary feeling of triumph, but when I saw the tiny wrinkles at the corners of Anne's eyes, and the fine lines round her mouth, I felt ashamed of myself. It was only too easy to follow my impulses and repent afterwards.

A week went by. Cyril and Elsa, who had no idea how matters were progressing, must have been expecting me every day. I was afraid to go and see them in case they tempted me to try anything new. Every afternoon I went up to my room, ostensibly to work, but in fact I did nothing: I had found a book on Yoga, and spent my time practising various exercises. I took care to smother my laughter in case Anne should hear it. I told her I was working hard; and I pretended that my disappointment in love had made me keen to get my degree as a consolation. I hoped this would raise me in her estimation, and I even went so far as to quote Kant at table, to my father's dismay.

One afternoon I had wrapped myself in bath towels to look like a Hindu, and was sitting cross-legged staring at myself in the mirror, hoping to achieve a Yoga-like trance, when there was a knock at the door. I thought it was the maid and told her to come in.

It was Anne. For a moment she remained transfixed in the doorway, then she smiled:

'What are you playing at?'

'Yoga,' I replied. 'But it's not a game at all, it's a Hindu philosophy.'

She went to the table and took up my book. I began to be alarmed. It lay open, and every page was covered with remarks in my handwriting, such as 'Impracticable', 'Exhausting'.

'You are certainly conscientious,' she said. 'And what about that essay on Pascal? I don't see it anywhere.'

At lunch I had been talking about Pascal, implying that I had worked on a certain passage, but needless to say I had not written a word. Anne waited for me to say something, but as I did not reply she understood.

'It is your own affair if you play the fool up here instead of working, but it's quite another matter when you lie to your father and me. In any case I found it difficult to believe in your sudden intellectual activity.'

She went out of the room leaving me petrified in my bath towels. I could not understand why she had used the word 'lie'. I had spoken of Pascal because it amused me, and had mentioned an essay to give her pleasure, and now she blamed me for it. I had grown used to her new attitude towards me, and her contempt made me feel humiliated and furious. I threw off my disguise, pulled on some slacks and an old shirt and rushed out of the house. The heat was terrific, but I began to run, impelled by my anger, which was all the more violent because it was mixed with shame. I ran all the way to Cyril's villa, only stopping when I reached the door to regain my breath. In the afternoon heat the houses seemed unnaturally large and quiet, and full of secrets. I went up to Cyril's room; he had shown it to me the day we visited his mother. I opened the door. He was lying across the bed, fast asleep with his head on his arm. I stood looking at him and for the first time he appeared to me defenceless and rather touching. I called him in a low voice. He opened his eyes and sat up at once.

'You, Cécile? What's the matter?'

I signed to him not to talk so loudly. Suppose his mother were to come and find me in his room? She might think . . . anyone might think . . . I suddenly felt panic-stricken and moved towards the door.

'But where are you off to?' he cried. 'Come here, Cécile!'

He caught me by the arm and laughingly held me back. I turned round to him, and saw him grow pale, as I must have been myself. He let go my wrist, only to take me in his arms, and draw me over to the bed. The thought that it had to happen sometime flashed through my confused mind.

I stayed with him for about an hour. I was happy, but bewildered. I was used to hearing the word love bandied about, and I had often mentioned it rather crudely as one does when one is young and ignorant, but now I felt I could never talk of it again in that detached and vulgar way. Cyril, lying beside me, was talking about marrying me and how we would be together always. My silence made him uneasy. I sat up, looked at him, and called him my lover. I kissed the vein on his neck, murmuring 'Darling, darling Cyril!' I was not sure whether it was love I felt for him at that moment, I have always been fickle, and I have no wish to delude myself on this point, but just then I loved him more than myself; I would have sacrificed my life for him. He asked me when I left if I was angry with him. I laughed: how could I possibly be angry?

I walked slowly back through the pine trees; I had asked Cyril not to come with me, it would have been too risky. In any case I was afraid something might show in my face or manner. Anne was lying in front of the house on a deck chair, reading. I had a story all ready to explain where I had been, but she said nothing, she never asked questions. Then I remembered that we had quarrelled, and I sat down near her in dead silence. I remained motionless, attentive to my own breathing and the trembling of my fingers, and thinking of Cyril.

I fetched a cigarette from the table and struck a match. It went out. With shaking hands I lighted another, and although there was no wind, it went out. In exasperation I took a third, and for some reason this match assumed a vital importance; perhaps because Anne was watching me intently. Suddenly everything around me seemed to melt away and there was nothing left but the match between my fingers, the box, and Anne's eyes boring into me. My heart was beating violently. I tightened my fingers round the match and struck it, but as I bent forward my cigarette put it out. The matchbox dropped to the ground and I could feel Anne's hard, searching gaze upon me. The tension was unbearable. Then her hands were under my chin, and as she raised my face I shut my eyes tightly for fear she should read their expression and see the tears welling up. She stroked my cheek and half reluctantly let me go, as if she preferred to leave the matter in abeyance. Then she put a lighted cigarette into my mouth and returned to her book.

Perhaps the incident was symbolic. Sometimes when I am groping for a match, I find myself thinking of that strange moment when my hands no longer seemed to belong to me, and once again I remember the intensity of Anne's look, and the emptiness around me.

5

The incident I have just described was not without its aftermath. Like certain people who are very self-controlled and sure of themselves, Anne would not make concessions; and when, on the terrace, she had let me go, she was acting against her principles. She had of course guessed something, and it would have been easy enough for her to make me talk, but at the last moment she had given in to pity or indifference. It was just as hard for her to make allowances for my shortcomings, as to try to improve them, in both cases she was merely prompted by a sense of duty; in marrying my father she felt she must also take charge of me. I would have found it easier to accept her constant disapproval if she had sometimes shown exasperation, or any other feeling which went more than skin deep. One gets used to other people's faults if one does not feel it a duty to correct them. Within a few months she would have ceased to trouble about me and her indifference might then have been tempered by affection. This attitude would just have suited me. But it could never happen with her, because her sense of responsibility was too strong, especially as I was young enough to be influenced; I was malleable, though obstinate.

Therefore she had a feeling of frustration where I was concerned, she was angry with herself, and she let me know it. A few days later we were at dinner when the controversial subject of my holiday task cropped up. I let myself go, and even my father showed annoyance, but in the end it was Anne who locked me up in my room, although she had not even raised her voice during the argument. I had no idea what she had done until I tried to leave the room to fetch a glass of water. I had never been locked up in my life, and at first I panicked. I rushed over to the window, but there was no escape that way. Then I threw myself against the door so violently that I bruised my shoulder. With my teeth clenched I tried to force the lock with a pair of tweezers, but I did not want to call anyone to open it. After that I stood still in the middle of the room and collected my thoughts, and gradually I became quite calm. It was my first experience of cruelty; the thought of it lay like a stone on my heart, until it formed the central point of my resistance. I sat on my bed and began to plan my revenge. Soon I was so engrossed that several times I went to the door, and was surprised to find that I could not get out.

At six o'clock my father came to release me. I got up when he came in, and smiled at him. He looked at me in silence.

'Do you want to talk to me?' he asked.

'What about?' I said. 'You know we both have a horror of explanations that lead nowhere.'

He seemed relieved: 'But do try to be nicer to Anne, more patient.'

I was taken aback. Why should he expect me to be patient with Anne? I suddenly realized that he thought of Anne as a woman he was imposing on me, instead of the contrary. There was evidently still room for hope.

'I was horrid,' I said. 'I'll apologize to her.'

'You're not unhappy, are you?'

'Of course not!' I replied. 'And anyhow if we quarrel too often, I shall just marry a little earlier, that's all!' I knew my words would strike home.

'You mustn't look at it in that way, you're not Snow-White!

Could you bear to leave me so soon? We should only have had two years together.'

The thought was as unbearable for me as for him. I could see myself crying on his shoulder, bewailing our lost happiness. I did not want to go too far.

'I'm exaggerating, you know. With a few concessions on both sides, Anne and I will get on all right.'

'Yes,' he said. 'Of course!'

He must have thought, as I did at that moment, that the concessions would probably not be mutual, but would be on my side only.

'You see,' I told him, 'I realize very well that Anne is always right. Her life is really far more successful than ours, and has greater depth.'

He started to protest, but I went on:

'In a month or two, I shall have completely assimilated Anne's ideas, and there won't be any more stupid arguments between us. It just needs patience.'

He was obviously startled. He was not only losing a boon companion, but a slice of his past as well.

'Now don't exaggerate!' he said in a weak voice. 'I know that the kind of life you have led with me was perhaps not suitable for your age, or mine either, for that matter, but it was neither dull nor unhappy. After all, we've never been bored or depressed during the last two years, have we? There's no need to be so drastic, just because Anne's conception of life is different.'

'On the contrary,' I said firmly. 'We'll have to go even further and give up our old way of life altogether!'

'I suppose so,' said my poor father as we went downstairs together.

I made my apologies to Anne without the slightest embarrassment. She told me that I needn't have bothered; the heat must have been the cause of our dispute. I felt gay and indifferent.

I met Cyril in the wood as arranged. I told him what to do next. He listened to me with a mixture of dread and admiration. Then he took me in his arms, but I could not stay, as it was getting late. I was surprised to find that I did not want to leave him. If he had been searching for some means of attaching me to himself, he had certainly found it. I kissed him passionately. I even longed to hurt him, so that he would not be able to forget me for a single moment all the evening, and dream of me all night long. I could not bear the thought of the night without him.

6

The next morning I took my father for a walk along the road. We talked gaily of insignificant things. I suggested going back to the villa by way of the pine wood. It was exactly half past ten; I was on time. My father walked in front of me on the narrow path and pushed aside the brambles, so that I should not scratch my legs. When he stopped dead in his tracks I knew he had seen them. I went up to him; Cyril and Elsa were lying apparently asleep on the pine needles. Although they were acting entirely on my instructions, and I knew very well that they were not in love, they were nevertheless both young and beautiful, and I could not help feeling a pang of jealousy. I noticed that my father had become abnormally pale. I took him by the arm:

'Don't let's disturb them. Come on!'

He glanced once more at Elsa, who was looking particularly pretty with her red hair spread out, and a half-smile on her lips: then he turned on his heel and walked on at a brisk pace. I could hear him muttering: 'The bitch! the bitch!'

'Why do you say that? She's free, isn't she?'

'That's not the point! Did you find it very pleasant to see her in Cyril's arms?'

'I don't love him any more,' I said.

'Neither do I love Elsa,' he answered furiously. 'But it hurts all the same. After all, I've lived with her, which makes it even worse.'

I knew very well what he meant. He must have felt like dashing up to separate them and seizing his property, or what had once been his property. 'Supposing Anne were to hear you?'

'What do you mean? Well, of course, she wouldn't understand, she'd be shocked, that's normal enough! But what about you? Don't YOU understand me any more? Are you shocked too?'

How easy it was for me to steer his thoughts in the direction I wanted! It was rather frightening to know him so well.

'Of course I'm not shocked,' I said. 'But you must see things as they are: Elsa has a short memory, she finds Cyril attractive, and that's the end of it as far as you're concerned. After all, look how you behaved to her, it was unforgivable!'

'If I wanted her . . .' my father began, and then stopped short.

'You'd have no luck,' I said convincingly, as if it were the most natural thing in the world for me to discuss his chances of getting Elsa back.

'Anyhow it is out of the question,' he said in a more resigned voice.

'Of course it is!' I answered with a shrug of my shoulders, which was meant to convey that he, poor chap, was out of the running now. He said not another word until we reached the house. Then he took Anne into his arms and held her close to him. She was surprised, but gladly submitted to his embrace. I went out of the room trembling with shame.

At two o'clock I heard a soft whistle, and went down to join Cyril on the beach. We got into the boat and sailed out to sea. There was nothing in sight, no one else was out in that heat. When we were some way from the shore, he lowered the sail. So far we had hardly exchanged a word.

'This morning . . .' he began.

'Please don't talk about it!' I said.

He gently pushed me down in the boat. I could feel it swaying

as we made love; the sky seemed to be falling on to us. I spoke
to him, but he made no reply, there was no need. Afterwards
there was the tang of salt water. We sunbathed, laughed and
were happy. We had the sun and the sea, laughter and love: I
wonder if we shall ever again recapture the particular flavour
and brilliance of those days, heightened as they were for me by
an undercurrent of fear and remorse?

The time passed quickly. I almost forgot Anne, my father, and
Elsa. Through love I had entered another world: I felt dreamy,
yet wide awake, peaceful, and contented. Cyril asked me if I
was not afraid. I told him that I was entirely his, and he seemed
satisfied that it should be so. Perhaps I had given myself to
him so easily because I knew that if I had a child, he would be
prepared to take the blame, and shoulder all the responsibility:
this was something I could never face. For once I was thankful
that my immaturity made it unlikely.

But Elsa was growing impatient. She plied me with questions. I was always afraid of being seen with her or Cyril. She
lay in wait for my father at every corner, and fondly imagined
that he had difficulty in keeping away from her. I was surprised
that someone who hovered so precariously between love and
money should get romantic ideas, and be excited by a look or
movement, when such things must otherwise have been merely
routine for her. The rôle she was playing evidently seemed to
her the height of psychological subtlety.

Even if my father was becoming gradually obsessed with the
thought of Elsa, Anne did not seem to notice it. He was more
affectionate and demonstrative than ever with her, which frightened me, because I attributed it to his subconscious remorse.
In three weeks we should be back in Paris, and the main thing
was that nothing should happen before then. Elsa would be out
of our way, and my father and Anne would get married if by
then they had not changed their minds. In Paris I would have

Cyril, and just as Anne had been unable to keep us apart here, so she would find it impossible to stop me from seeing him once we were home. Cyril had a room of his own away from his mother's house. I could already picture ourselves there together, the window wide open to the wonderful pink and blue sky of Paris, pigeons cooing on the bars outside, and Cyril with me on the narrow bed.

7

A few days later my father received a message from one of our friends asking us to meet him in Saint-Raphaël for a drink. He was so pleased at the thought of escaping for a while from the unnatural seclusion in which we were living that he could hardly wait to tell us the news. I mentioned to Elsa and Cyril that we would be at the Bar du Soleil at seven o'clock and if they liked to come, they would see us there. Unfortunately, Elsa happened to know our friend, which made her all the more keen to go. I realized that there might be complications, and tried in vain to put her off.

'Charles Webb simply adores me,' she said with childlike simplicity. 'If he sees me, he's sure to make Raymond want to come back to me.'

Cyril did not care whether he went to Saint-Raphaël or not. I saw by the way he looked at me that he only wanted to be near me, and I felt proud.

At six o'clock we drove off in Anne's car. It was a huge American 'convertible', which she kept more for publicity than to suit her own taste, but it suited mine down to the ground, with all its shining gadgets. Another advantage was that we could all three sit in front, and I never feel so friendly as when I am in a car, sharing the same pleasures, and perhaps even the same death. Anne was at the wheel, as if symbolizing her future place in the family. This was the first time I had been in her car since the evening we went to Cannes.

We met Charles Webb and his wife at the Bar du Soleil. He was concerned with theatrical publicity, while his wife spent all his earnings on entertaining young men. Money was an obsession with him, he thought of nothing else in his unceasing effort to make ends meet; hence his restless impatience. He had been Elsa's lover for a long time, and she had suited him quite well, because, though very pretty, she was not particularly grasping.

His wife was a malicious woman. Anne had never met her, and I noticed that her lovely face quickly assumed the disdainful, mocking expression that was habitual to her in society. As usual Charles Webb talked all the time, now and then giving Anne an inquisitive look. He evidently wondered what she was doing with that Don Juan Raymond and his daughter. I was glad to think he would soon find out. Just then my father leant forward and said abruptly:

'I have news for you, old chap: Anne and I are getting married on the 5th of October.'

Webb looked from one to the other in amazement; his wife, who had rather a weakness for my father, seemed disconcerted.

After a pause, Webb shouted: 'Congratulations! What a splendid idea! My dear lady, you don't know what you're taking on, you are wonderful! Here, waiter! We must celebrate.'

Anne smiled quietly and indifferently. Then I saw Webb's face light up, and I did not turn round:

'Elsa! Good Heavens, it's Elsa Mackenbourg! She hasn't seen me yet. I say, Raymond, do you see how lovely that girl has grown?'

'Hasn't she!' said my father in a proprietary voice, but then he remembered and his face fell.

Anne could hardly help noticing the inflection in his voice. She turned to me with a quick movement, but before she could speak I leant towards her and said in a confidential whisper, loud enough for my father to hear:

'Anne, you're causing quite a sensation. There's a man over there who can't take his eyes off you.'

My father twisted round to look at the man in question:

'I won't have this sort of thing!' he said, taking Anne's hand.

'Aren't they sweet?' exclaimed Madame Webb, ironically. 'Charles, we really shouldn't have disturbed them; it would have been better to have invited Cécile by herself.'

'She wouldn't have come,' I said unhesitatingly.

'Why not? Are you in love with one of the fishermen?'

She had once seen me in conversation with a bus conductor, and ever since had treated me as though I had lost caste.

'Why yes, of course!' I said with an effort to appear gay.

'And do you go out fishing a lot?'

She thought she was being funny, which made it even worse. I was beginning to get angry, but did not know what to answer without being too offensive. There was dead silence. Anne's voice interposed quietly:

'Raymond, would you mind asking the waiter to bring me a straw to drink my orange juice?'

Charles Webb began to talk feverishly about refreshing drinks. Anne gave me a look of entreaty. We all decided to dine together as though we had narrowly escaped a scene.

At dinner I drank far too much. I wanted to forget Anne's anxious expression when she looked at my father, and the hint of gratitude in her eyes whenever they rested on me. Every time Madame Webb made a dig at me I gave her an ingratiating smile. This seemed to upset her, and she soon became openly aggressive. Anne signed to me to keep quiet, she had a horror of scenes in public, and Madame Webb seemed to be on the point of creating one. For my part I was used to them. Among our associates they were frequent, so I was not disturbed by the prospect.

After dinner we went to another bar. Soon Elsa and Cyril turned up. Elsa was talking very loudly as she entered the room followed by poor Cyril. I thought she was behaving badly, but she was pretty enough to carry it off.

'Who's that puppy she's with?' asked Charles Webb. 'He's rather young, isn't he?'

'It's love that keeps him young!' simpered his wife.

'Don't you believe it!' said my father. 'It's just an infatuation.'

I had my eyes on Anne. She was watching Elsa in the calm, detached way she looked at very young women, or at the mannequins parading her collection. For a moment I admired her passionately for showing no trace of jealousy or spite, but how could she be jealous, I wondered, when she herself was a hundred times more beautiful and intelligent than Elsa? As I was very drunk, I told her so. She looked at me curiously:

'Do you really think I am more beautiful than Elsa?'

'Of course!'

'That is always pleasant to hear, but you are drinking too much. Give me your glass. I hope it doesn't upset you to see Cyril here? Anyway he seems bored to death.'

'He's my lover,' I said with gay abandon.

'You are quite drunk. Fortunately it's time to go home.'

It was a relief to part from the Webbs. I found it difficult to say goodbye politely. My father drove, and my head lolled on to Anne's shoulder.

I began to reflect how much I preferred her to the people we usually saw, that she was infinitely superior to them in every way. My father said very little, perhaps he was thinking of Elsa.

'Is she sleeping?' he asked Anne.

'As peacefully as a baby. She didn't behave badly on the whole, did she?'

They were silent for a while, then I heard his voice again:

'Anne, I love you; only you. Do you believe me?'

'Don't tell me so often, it frightens me.'

'Give me your hand.'

I almost sat up to protest: 'For heaven's sake, not on the Corniche!', but I was too drunk, and half asleep. Besides there was Anne's perfume, the sea breeze in my hair, the tiny graze on my shoulder which was a reminder of Cyril; all these reasons to be happy and keep quiet. I thought of Elsa and Cyril setting off on the motor cycle which had been a birthday present from his mother. I felt so sorry for them that I almost cried. Anne's car was made for sleeping, so well sprung, not noisy like a motor bike. I thought of Madame Webb lying awake at night. No doubt at her age I would also have to pay someone to love me, because love is the most wonderful thing in the world. What does the price matter? The important thing was not to become embittered and jealous, as she was of Elsa and Anne. I began to laugh softly to myself. Anne moved her shoulder to make a comfortable hollow for me. 'Go to sleep,' she ordered. I went to sleep.

8

The next morning I woke up feeling perfectly well except for a slight ache in my neck. My bed was flooded with sunshine as it was every morning. I threw back the sheets and exposed my bare back to the sun. It was warm and comforting, and seemed to penetrate my very bones. I decided to spend the morning like that, without moving.

In my mind I went over the events of the evening before. I remembered telling Anne that Cyril was my lover. It amused me to think that one can tell the truth when one is drunk and nobody will believe it. I thought about Madame Webb. I was used to that sort of woman: in her milieu and at her age they often become odious through their self-indulgence; Anne's calm dignity had shown her up as even more idiotic and boring than usual. It was only to be expected; I could not imagine anyone among my father's friends who would for a moment bear comparison with Anne. In order to be able to face an evening with people like that, one had either to be rather drunk, or be on intimate terms with one or other of them. For my father it was more simple: Charles Webb and he were libertines: 'Guess whom I'm taking out tonight? The Mars girl, the one in Saurel's latest film.' My father would laugh, and clap him on the back: 'Lucky man! She's almost as pretty as Élise.' Undergraduate talk, but I liked their enthusiasm.

Then there were interminable evenings on café terraces, and

Lombard's tales of woe: 'She was the only one I ever loved, Raymond! Do you remember that spring before she left me? It's stupid for a man to devote his whole life to one woman.' This was another side of life.

Anne's friends probably never talked about themselves, perhaps they did not indulge in such adventures. Or if they spoke of them, it must be with an apologetic laugh. Already I almost shared Anne's condescending attitude towards our friends: it was catching. On the other hand, by the age of thirty, I could imagine myself being more like them than like Anne, and by then her silence, indifference and reserve might suffocate me. There was a knock at the door. I quickly put on my pyjama top and called 'Come in!' Anne stood there, carefully holding a cup.

'I thought you might like some coffee. How do you feel this morning?'

'Very well,' I answered. 'I'm afraid I was a bit tipsy last night.'

'As you are each time you go out,' she began to laugh. 'But I must say, you were amusing. It was such a tedious evening.'

I had forgotten the sun, and even my coffee. When I was talking to Anne, I was completely absorbed; I did not think of myself, and yet she was the only one who made me question my motives. Through her I lived more intensely.

'Cécile, do you find people like the Webbs and the Dupuis entertaining?'

'Well, they usually behave abominably, but they are funny.'

She was watching a fly on the floor. Anne's eyelids were long and heavy; it was easy for her to look condescending.

'Don't you ever realize how monotonous and dull their conversation is? Don't those endless stories about girls, contracts and parties bore you?'

'I'm afraid,' I answered, 'that after ten years of convent life their lack of morals fascinates me.'

I did not dare to add that I also liked it.

'You left two years ago,' she said. 'It's not anything one can reason about, neither is it a question of morals; it has something to do with one's sensibility, a sixth sense.'

I supposed I hadn't got it. I saw clearly that I was lacking in this respect.

'Anne,' I asked abruptly, 'do you think I am intelligent?'

She began to laugh, surprised at the directness of my question.

'Of course you are! Why do you ask?'

'If I were an idiot, you'd say just the same thing,' I sighed. 'I so often find your superiority overpowering.'

'It's just a question of age,' she answered. 'It would be a sad thing if I didn't feel a little more self-assured than you.'

She laughed. I was annoyed:

'It wouldn't necessarily be a bad thing.'

'It would be a catastrophe,' she said.

She suddenly dropped her bantering tone and looked me straight in the face. I at once felt ill-at-ease, and began to fidget. Even today I cannot get used to people who stare at you while they are talking, or come very close to make quite sure that you are listening. My only thought then is to escape from such proximity. I go on saying 'Yes', while gradually edging away; their insistence and indiscretion enrage me. What right have they to try to corner me? Fortunately, Anne did not resort to these tactics, but merely kept her eyes fixed on me, so that I could no longer continue to talk in the light-hearted vein I usually affected.

'Do you know how men like Webb end up?'

I thought: 'And men like my father.'

'In the river,' I answered flippantly.

'A time comes when they are no longer attractive or in good form. They can't drink any more, and they still hanker after women, only then they have to pay and make compromises in order to escape from their loneliness: they have become just figures of fun. They grow sentimental and hard to please. I have seen many who have gone the same way.'

'Poor Webb!' I said.

I was impressed. So that was the fate in store for my father? Or at least the fate from which Anne was saving him.

'You never thought of that, did you?' said Anne, with a little smile of commiseration. 'You don't think much about the future, do you? That is the privilege of youth.'

'Please don't throw my youth at me like that! I use it neither as an excuse, nor as a privilege. I just don't attach any importance to it.'

'To what do you attach importance? To your peace of mind? Your independence?'

I dreaded conversations of this sort, especially with Anne.

'To nothing at all,' I said. 'You know I hardly ever think.'

'You and your father irritate me at times: "You haven't given it a thought . . . you're not up to much . . . you don't know." Are you satisfied to be like that?'

'I'm not satisfied with myself. I don't like myself, and I don't try to. At moments you force me to complicate my life, and I almost hate you for it.'

She began to hum to herself with a thoughtful expression. I recognized the tune, but did not know what it was:

'What's the name of that song, Anne? It gets on my nerves.'

'I don't know,' she smiled again, looking rather discouraged.

'Stay in bed and rest, I'll continue my research on the family intellect somewhere else.'

I thought it was easy enough for my father. I could just imagine him saying 'I'm not thinking of anything special because I love you, Anne.' However intelligent she was, Anne would accept this as a valid excuse. I gave myself a good stretch and lay down on my pillow. Anne was dramatizing the situation: in twenty-five years my father would be an amiable sexagenarian with white hair, rather addicted to whisky and highly-coloured reminiscences. We would go out together; it would be my turn to tell him my adventures, and his to advise me. I realized that in my mind I was excluding Anne from our future: I did not see how she could fit in. Amidst the turmoil of our flat, which was sometimes bare, at others full of flowers, the stage for many and varied scenes, often cluttered up with luggage, I somehow could not envisage the introduction of order, the peace and quiet, the feeling of harmony that Anne brought with her everywhere she went, as if they were the most precious gifts. I dreaded being bored to death; although I was less apprehensive of her influence since my love for Cyril had liberated me from many of my fears. I feared boredom and tranquillity more than anything. In order to achieve serenity, my father and I had to have excitement, and this Anne was not prepared to admit.

9

I have spoken a great deal about Anne and myself, and very little of my father. Yet he has played the most important part in this story, and my feelings for him have been deeper and more stable than for anyone else. I know him too well, and feel too close to him to talk easily of him, and it is he above all others whom I wish to justify and present in a good light. He was neither vain nor selfish, but incurably frivolous. I could not call him irresponsible or incapable of deep feelings. His love for me is not to be taken lightly or regarded merely as a parental habit. He could suffer more through me than through anyone else, and for my part I was nearer to despair the day he turned away as if abandoning me than I had ever been in my life. I was always more important to him than his love affairs. On certain evenings, by taking me home, he must have missed what his friend Webb would have called 'great opportunities'. On the other hand, I cannot deny that he was unfaithful and would always take the easiest way. He never reflected, and tried to give everything a physiological explanation which he called being rational: 'You think yourself hateful? Sleep more and drink less!' It was the same when at times he had a violent desire for a particular woman. He never thought of repressing it, or trying to elevate it into a complex sentiment. He was a materialist, but kind and understanding and had a touch of delicacy. His desire for Elsa disturbed him, but not in the way one might expect. He did not say to himself: 'I want to be unfaithful to Anne, therefore I love her less,' but 'This need for Elsa is a nuisance, I must get over it quickly or it might cause complications with Anne.' Moreover he loved and admired Anne. She was a change from the stupid and frivolous women he had consorted with in recent years. She satisfied his vanity, his sensuality and his sensibility, for she understood him, and offered her intelligence and experience to supplement his. But I do not believe he realized how deeply she cared for him. He thought of her as the ideal mistress and an ideal mother for me, but I do not think he visualized her as the ideal wife for himself, with all this implied. I am sure that in Cyril's and in Anne's eyes he was like me, abnormal, so to speak; but although he considered his life banal, he put all his vitality into it and made it exciting.

I was not thinking of him when I formed the project of shutting Anne out of our lives; I knew he would console himself as he always did: a clean break with Anne would in the long run be less painful than living a well-regulated life as her husband. What really destroyed him, as it did me, was being subjected to fixed habits. We were of the same race; sometimes I thought we belonged to the pure and beautiful race of nomads, and at others to the poor withered breed of hedonists.

At that moment he was suffering, or at least he was feeling exasperated: Elsa had become the symbol of his past life and of youth, above all his own youth. I knew he was dying to say to Anne: 'Dearest, let me go for just one day; I must prove to myself with Elsa's help that I'm not an old fogey.' But that was impossible; not because Anne was jealous, or too virtuous to discuss such matters, but because she had made up her mind to live with him on her own terms. She was determined to put an end to the era of frivolity and debauch and to stop him behaving like a schoolboy. She was entrusting her life to him and in future he must behave well and not be a slave to his caprices. One could not blame Anne: hers was a perfectly normal and sensible point of view, but it did not prevent my father from wanting Elsa – from desiring her more and more as time passed and his feeling of frustration increased.

At that moment I have no doubt that I could have arranged everything. I had only to tell Elsa to go and meet him and resume their former relations, and I could easily have persuaded Anne to go with me to Nice on some pretext. On our return we would have found my father relaxed, and filled with a new taste for legalized affections, or rather, those shortly to become legalized. But Anne could not have borne the idea of having been merely a mistress like the others. How difficult she made life for us through the high esteem in which she held herself!

But I said nothing to Elsa, neither did I ask Anne to go to Nice with me. I wanted my father's desire to fester in him, so that in the end he would give himself away. I could not bear the contempt with which Anne treated our past life, her disdain for what had been our happiness. I had no wish to humiliate her, but only to force her to accept our way of life. For this it was necessary that she should discover his infidelity, and should see it objectively as a passing fancy, not as an attack on her personal dignity. If at all cost she wished to be in the right, she must allow us to be in the wrong.

I even pretended not to notice my father's plight. On no account could I become his accomplice by speaking to Elsa for him, or getting Anne out of the way. I had to pretend to look upon Anne and his love for her as sacred, and I must admit it was not difficult for me. The idea that he could be unfaithful and defy her filled me with terror and a vague admiration.

In the meanwhile we had many happy days. I made use of every occasion to further my father's interest in Elsa. The sight of Anne's face no longer filled me with remorse. I sometimes imagined that she would accept everything, and that we would be able to live a life that suited us all three equally well. I often saw Cyril, and we made love in secret. The scent of the pines, and the sound of the sea added to the enchantment. He began to torment himself; he hated the rôle I had forced upon him, and only continued with it because I made him believe it was necessary for our love. All this involved a great deal of deceit, and much had to be concealed, but it did not cost me much effort to tell a few lies, and after all, I alone controlled, and was the sole judge of my actions.

I will pass quickly over this period, for I am afraid that if I look at it closely, I shall revive memories that are too painful. Already I feel overwhelmed as I think of Anne's happy laugh, of her kindness to me. My conscience troubles me so much at those moments that I am obliged to resort to some expedient like lighting a cigarette, putting on a record, or telephoning to a friend. Then gradually I begin to think of something else. But I do not like having to take refuge in forgetfulness and frivolity instead of facing my memories and fighting them.

IO

Destiny sometimes assumes strange forms. That summer it appeared in the guise of Elsa, a mediocre person, but with a pretty face. She had an extraordinary laugh, sudden and infectious, which only rather stupid people possess.

I soon noticed the effect of this laugh on my father. I told her to make the utmost use of it whenever we 'surprised' her with Cyril. My orders were: 'When you hear me coming with my father, say nothing, just laugh.' And at the sound of that laugh a look of fury would come into my father's face. My rôle of stage manager continued to be exciting. I never missed my mark, for when we saw Cyril and Elsa openly showing signs of an imaginary relationship my father and I both grew pale with the violence of our feelings. The sight of Cyril bending over Elsa made my heart ache. I would have given anything in that world to stop them, forgetting that it was I who had planned it.

Apart from these incidents and filling our daily life were Anne's confidence, gentleness and (I hate to use the word) happiness. She was nearer to happiness than I had ever seen her since she had been at our mercy, egoists that we were. She was far removed from our violent desires and my base little schemes. I had counted on her aloofness and instinctive pride preventing her from making any special effort to attach my father to her, and that she would rely on looking beautiful, and being her intelligent, loving self.

I began to feel sorry for her, and pity is an agreeable sentiment, moving, like military music.

One fine morning the maid, in great excitement, handed me a note from Elsa: 'All is well. Come!' I had an impression of imminent catastrophe: I hate final scenes. I met Elsa on the beach, looking triumphant.

'At last I managed to speak to your father, just an hour ago.'

'What did he say?'

'He told me he was very sorry for what had happened, that he had behaved like a cad. It's the truth, isn't it?'

I thought it best to agree.

'Then he paid me compliments in the way only he can, you know, rather detached, in a low voice, as if at the same time it hurt him.'

I interrupted her: 'What was he leading up to?'

'Well, nothing. Oh yes, he asked me to have tea with him in the village to show there was no ill-feeling, and that I was broad-minded. Shall I go?'

My father's views on the broad-mindedness of red-haired girls were a treat. I felt like saying that it had nothing to do with me. Then I realized that she held me responsible for her success. Rightly or wrongly, it irritated me. I felt trapped.

'I don't know, Elsa. That depends on you. You always ask me what you should do, one might almost believe that it was I who forced you . . .'

'But it was you,' she said. 'It's entirely through you that . . .'

The admiration in her voice suddenly frightened me:

'Go if you want to, but for heaven's sake, don't say any more about it!'

'But Cécile, isn't the whole idea to free him from that woman's clutches?'

I fled. Let my father do as he wished, and Anne must deal with it as best she could. Anyhow I was on my way to meet

Cyril. It seemed to me that love was the only remedy for the haunting fear I felt.

Cyril took me in his arms without a word. Once I was with him, everything became quite simple. Later, lying beside him, I told him that I hated myself. I smiled as I said it because although I meant it, there was no pain, only a pleasant resignation. He did not take me seriously:

'What does it matter? I love you so much that I shall make you feel as I do.'

All through our midday meal I thought of his words: 'I love you so much.' That is why, although I have tried hard, I cannot remember much about that lunch. Anne was wearing a mauve dress, as mauve as the shadows under her eyes; the colour of her eyes themselves. My father laughed, and was evidently well pleased with himself: everything was going well for him. During dessert he announced that he had some shopping to do in the village that afternoon. I smiled to myself. I was tired of the whole thing, and felt fatalistic about it. My one desire was to have a swim.

At four o'clock I went down to the beach. I saw my father on the terrace about to leave for the village; I did not speak, not even to warn him to be careful.

The water was soft and warm. Anne did not appear. I supposed she was busy in her room designing her next collection, and meanwhile my father was making the most of his time with Elsa. After two hours, when I was tired of sunbathing, I went up to the terrace and sitting down in a chair, opened a newspaper.

At that moment Anne appeared from the direction of the wood. She was running, clumsily, heavily, her elbows close to her sides. I had a sudden, ghastly impression of an old woman running towards me, and that she was about to fall down. I did not move; she disappeared behind the house near the garage. In a flash I understood, and I too began running to catch her.

She was already in her car starting it up. I rushed over and clutched at the door.

'Anne,' I cried. 'Don't go, it's all a mistake, it's my fault. I'll explain everything.'

She paid no attention to me, but bent to take the brake off.

'Anne, we need you!'

She straightened up, and I saw that her face was distorted; she was crying. Then I realized that I had attacked a living, sensitive creature, not just an entity. She too must once have been a rather secretive little girl, then an adolescent, and after that a woman. Now she was forty, and all alone. She loved a man, and had hoped to spend ten or twenty happy years with him. As for me . . . that poor miserable face was my work. I was petrified; I trembled all over as I leant against the door.

'You have no need of anyone,' she murmured. 'Neither you nor he.'

The engine was running. I was desperate, she couldn't go like that!

'Forgive me! I beg you . . .'

'Forgive you? What for?'

The tears were streaming down her face. She did not seem to notice them.

'My poor child!'

She laid her hand against my cheek for a moment, then drove away. I saw her car disappearing round the side of the house. I was irretrievably lost. It had all happened so quickly. I thought of her face.

I heard steps behind me: it was my father. He had taken the time to remove the imprint of Elsa's lipstick from his face, and brush the pine needles from his suit. I turned round and threw myself on him.

'You beast!'

I began to sob.

'But what's the matter? Where is Anne? Cécile, tell me, Cécile!'

11

We did not meet again until dinner. Both of us were nervous at being suddenly alone together, and neither he nor I had any appetite. We realized it was necessary to get Anne back. I could not bear to think of the look of horror on her face before she left, of her distress and my own responsibility. All my cunning manoeuvres and carefully laid plans were forgotten. I was thrown completely off my balance, and I could see from his expression that my father felt the same.

'Do you think,' he said, 'that she'll stay away from us for long?'

'I expect she's gone to Paris,' I said.

'Paris,' murmured my father in a dreamy voice.

'Perhaps we shall never see her again.'

He seemed at a loss for words, and took my hand across the table.

'You must be terribly angry with me. I don't know what came over me. On the way back through the woods I kissed Elsa, and just at that moment Anne must have arrived.'

I was not listening. The figures of Elsa and my father embracing under the pines seemed theatrical and unreal to me, and I could not visualize them. The only vivid memory of that day was my last glimpse of Anne's face with its look of grief and betrayal.

I took a cigarette from my father's packet and lit it. Smoking during meals was a thing Anne could not bear.

I smiled at my father:

'I understand very well, it's not your fault. It was a momentary lapse, as they say. But we must get Anne to forgive us, or rather you.'

'What shall we do?' he asked me.

He looked far from well. I felt sorry for him and for myself too. After all, what was Anne up to, leaving us in the lurch like that, making us suffer for one moment of folly? Hadn't she a duty towards us?

'Let's write to her,' I said. 'And ask her forgiveness.'

'What a wonderful idea,' said my father.

At last he had found some means of escape from the stupor and remorse of the past three hours. Without waiting to finish our meal, we pushed back the cloth, my father went to fetch a lamp, pens, and some notepaper; we sat down opposite each other, almost smiling because our preparations had made Anne's return seem probable. A bat was circling round outside the window. My father started writing.

An unbearable feeling of disgust and horror rises in me when I think of the letters full of fine sentiments we wrote that evening, sitting under the lamp like two awkward schoolchildren, applying ourselves in silence to the impossible task of getting Anne back. However we managed to produce two works of art, full of excuses, love, and repentance. When I had finished, I felt almost certain that Anne would not be able to resist us, and that a reconciliation was imminent. I could already imagine the scene as she forgave us, it would take place in our drawing-room in Paris, Anne would come in and . . .

At that moment the telephone rang. It was ten o'clock. We exchanged a look of astonishment which soon turned to hope; it was Anne telephoning to say she forgave us and was returning. My father bounded to the telephone and called 'Hello' in a voice full of joy.

Then he said nothing but 'Yes, yes, where is that? yes' in an almost inaudible whisper. I got up, shaken by fear. My father passed his hand over his face with a mechanical gesture. At length he gently replaced the receiver and turned to me:

'She has had an accident,' he said. 'On the road to Estérel. It took them some time to discover her address. They telephoned to Paris and got our number from there.'

He went on in the same flat voice, and I dared not interrupt:

'The accident happened at the most dangerous spot. There have been many at that place, it seems. The car fell down fifty metres. It would have been a miracle if she had escaped.'

The rest of that night I remember as if it had been a nightmare: the road surging up under the headlights, my father's stony face, the door of the clinic. My father would not let me see her. I sat on a bench in the waiting-room staring at a lithograph of Venice. I thought of nothing. A nurse told me that this was the sixth accident at that place since the beginning of the summer. My father did not come back.

Then I thought that once again by her death Anne had proved herself different from us. If we had wanted to commit suicide, even supposing we had the courage, it would have been with a bullet in the head, leaving an explanatory note destined to trouble the sleep of those who were responsible. But Anne had made us the magnificent present of giving us the chance to believe in an accident. A dangerous place on the road, a car that easily lost balance. It was a gift that we would soon be weak enough to accept. In any case it is a romantic idea of mine to call it suicide. Can one commit suicide on account of people like my father and myself, people who have no need of anybody, living or dead? My father and I never spoke of it as anything but an accident.

The next day we returned to the house at about three o'clock in the afternoon. Elsa and Cyril were waiting for us, sitting on the steps. They seemed like two comic, forgotten characters; neither of them had known Anne, or loved her. There they were with their little love affairs, their good looks, and their embarrassment. Cyril came up to me and put his hand on my arm. I looked at him: I had never loved him. I had found him gentle and attractive. I had loved the pleasure he gave me, but I did not need him. I was going away, leaving behind me the house, the garden, and that summer. My father was with me; he took my arm and we went indoors.

In the house were Anne's jacket, her flowers, her room, her scent. My father closed the shutters, took a bottle out of the refrigerator and fetched two glasses. It was the only remedy to hand. Our letters of excuse still lay on the table. I pushed them off and they floated to the floor. My father, who was coming towards me holding a full glass, hesitated, then, avoided them. I found it symbolical. I took my glass and drained it in one gulp. The room was in half darkness, I saw my father's shadow on the window. The sea was beating on the shore.

12

The funeral took place in Paris on a fine day. There was the usual curious crowd dressed in black. My father and I shook hands with Anne's elderly relations. I looked at them with interest: they would probably have come to tea with us once a year. People commiserated with my father. Webb must have spread the news of his intended marriage. I saw that Cyril was looking for me after the service, but I avoided him. The resentment I felt towards him was quite unjustified, but I could not help it. Everyone was deploring the dreadful and senseless event, and as I was still rather doubtful whether it had been an accident, I was relieved.

In the car on the way back, my father took my hand and held it tightly. I thought: 'Now we have only each other, we are alone and unhappy,' and for the first time I cried. My tears were some comfort, they were not at all like the terrible emptiness I had felt in the clinic in front of the picture of Venice. My father gave me his handkerchief without a word, his face was ravaged.

For a month we lived like a widower and an orphan, eating all our meals together and staying at home. Sometimes we spoke of Anne: 'Do you remember the day when . . . ?' We chose our words with care, and averted our eyes for fear we might hurt each other, or that something irreparable would come between us. Our discretion and restraint brought their own recompense. Soon we could speak of Anne in a normal way as of a person dear to us, with whom we could have been happy, but whom God had called to Himself. God instead of chance. We did not believe in God. In these circumstances we were thankful to believe in fate.

Then one day at a friend's house I met a young man I liked and who liked me. For a week I went out with him constantly, and my father, who could not bear to be alone, followed my example with an ambitious young woman. Life began to take its old course, as it was bound to. When my father and I were alone together we joked, and discussed our latest conquests. He must suspect that my friendship with Philippe is not platonic, and I know very well that his new friend is costing him too much money. But we are happy. Winter is drawing to an end; we shall not rent the same villa again, but another one, near Juan-les-Pins.

Only when I am in bed, at dawn, listening to the cars passing below in the streets of Paris, my memory betrays me: that summer returns to me with all its memories. Anne, Anne, I repeat over and over again softly in the darkness. Then something rises in me that I welcome by name, with closed eyes: Bonjour tristesse!

A Certain Smile

À Florence Malraux

PART ONE

*L'amour c'est ce qui se passe
entre deux personnes
qui s'aiment*

ROGER VAILLAND

I

We had spent the afternoon in a café in the Rue Saint-Jacques, a spring afternoon like any other. I was slightly bored, and walked up and down between the juke-box and the window, while Bertrand talked about Spire's lecture. I was leaning on the machine, watching the record rising slowly, almost gently, like a proffered cheek, to its slanting position against the sapphire, when, for no apparent reason, I was overcome by a feeling of intense happiness, a sudden realization that some day I would die, that my hand would no longer touch that chromium rim, nor would the sun shine in my eyes.

I turned towards Bertrand; when he saw me smile he got up. He could not bear me to be happy without him. My joys were to be limited to the short and most important moments of our life together. In a vague way I already knew this, but that day I could not tolerate it, and turned back to the machine. The piano was playing the theme of 'Lone and Sweet' and the clarinet took it up. Every note of the tune was familiar.

I had met Bertrand the previous year during the examinations. We had passed an agonizing week side by side before I left to spend the summer with my parents. The last evening he kissed me, then came his letters. Casual at first; after that the tone changed. I followed their progress with a certain emotion, so that when he wrote: 'It sounds a ridiculous declaration, but I think I'm in love with you,' I was able to answer in the same vein without lying: 'Your declaration is ridiculous, but I love you too.' My reply came to me quite naturally, or rather, like an echo.

My parents' property on the River Yonne offered few distractions. I would go down to the river-bank, look for a moment at the weeds floating yellow and undulating on the surface, then choose little flattened stones to send skimming over the water like black, darting swallows. All that summer I repeated to myself the name Bertrand, and thought of the future. In a certain way it appealed to me to begin a love affair by correspondence.

Bertrand now came up behind me. He offered me my glass and when I turned round I found him close to me. He was always annoyed when I was inattentive during those interminable discussions he had with his friends. I was rather fond of reading, but literary talk bored me. He could not get accustomed to this.

'You always put on the same tune; though, mind you, I quite like it,' he said.

He lowered his voice on the last words which reminded me that we were together the first time we heard the record. I always noticed his little sentimental allusions to various landmarks in our relationship which I had quite forgotten. 'He means nothing to me,' I thought; 'he bores me, I'm indifferent to all this, I am nothing, nothing, absolutely nothing!' And the same absurd feeling of elation got hold of me.

'I have to go and see my uncle, the great traveller,' said Bertrand. 'Coming?'

He went out and I followed. I did not know his uncle and did not want to. But there was something in me that seemed destined to follow the well-shaved neck of a young man, always letting myself be led along unresistingly, except for the icy little thoughts that swam through my mind like fish. I felt a certain affection for him just then. As we walked along the boulevard our feet kept time like our bodies at night. He held my hand. We were slim and pleasing, like people in a picture.

All along the boulevard and on the platform of the bus taking us to his uncle I went on feeling very fond of Bertrand. I was pushed against him by the surge of people. He laughed and put a protecting arm round me. I leaned against his jacket by the curve of his shoulder, that masculine shoulder so comfortable for my head. I inhaled his perfume which I knew well, and it moved me. He had been my only lover. It was through him I had learnt to know my own body. It is always through the body of another that one discovers one's own, at first with suspicion and then with gratitude.

Bertrand talked about his uncle; he did not seem to care much for him. He made fun of his travels, for Bertrand spent his time looking for a reason to ridicule others, to such an extent that he lived in constant fear that one day he might unknowingly appear ridiculous himself. The fact that this struck me as absurd made him furious.

Bertrand's uncle was waiting for him on the terrace of a café. When I caught sight of him I remarked to Bertrand that he didn't look at all bad. As we came near he got up.

'Luc,' said Bertrand, 'I've brought a friend. Dominique, this is my Uncle Luc, the famous traveller.'

I was agreeably surprised, and thought: 'He looks quite passable.' He had grey eyes and a tired, almost sad expression. In a way he was handsome.

'How did the last journey go off?' said Bertrand.

'Very badly. I had to wind up a tedious legal affair in Boston. There were tiresome little lawyers in every corner. An awful bore. And you?'

'Our exam is in two months,' said Bertrand.

He had emphasized 'our'. This was the conjugal aspect of the Sorbonne; one spoke of examinations as one would of babies. Bertrand's uncle turned to me:

'Do you pass exams too?'

'Yes,' I answered vaguely. I was always rather ashamed of my modest activities.

'I've run out of cigarettes,' said Bertrand.

I watched him as he got up. His walk was quick and supple. Whenever I thought that this combination of muscles, reflexes, and olive skin belonged to me, it always seemed an astonishing gift.

'What do you do apart from exams?' asked Bertrand's uncle.

'Nothing,' I said; 'well, nothing much.'

I raised my hand as if to suggest futility. He caught it in mid-air and I looked at him surprised. The thought flashed through my mind: 'He's attractive, he's rather old, but he attracts me.' He laid my hand on the table, smiling:

'Your fingers are all ink-stained, it's a good sign. You'll pass your exams and be a brilliant lawyer, although you don't appear to be very talkative . . .'

We both laughed. I told myself that I must make a friend of him.

But already Bertrand was coming back. Luc was talking to him but I did not listen. Luc had a slow way of speaking and large hands. I thought: 'He's just the type who tries to seduce young girls like me.' I determined to be on my guard, but still I could not help feeling a pang of disappointment when he invited us to lunch two days later, but with his wife.

2

Before we had lunch at Luc's I passed two rather dull days. What did I really do with myself? I worked half-heartedly for an examination that would not lead very far, basked in the sun, and accepted Bertrand's love; for though I was fond of him I did not give him much in return. It seemed to me that mutual confidence, affection, and esteem were not to be despised, and I seldom thought about passion. After all, most people appear to live without very deep emotions. One must make the most of what life offers, and that, I found, was difficult enough.

I lived in a sort of family pension, only occupied by students. The management was not strict, and I could easily stay out until one or two o'clock in the morning, My room had a low ceiling, and was large and completely bare, as I had soon dropped my original plan to redecorate it. I asked only that my surroundings should be unobtrusive. The house had a provincial atmosphere which I liked very much. My window faced a courtyard bounded by a low wall over which one caught glimpses of the Paris sky, carved into pathetic triangles above the streets and balconies.

I got up in the morning to go to lectures, and met Bertrand for lunch. There was the library at the Sorbonne; there were cinemas, café terraces, friends, and work. In the evening we went dancing or returned to Bertrand's room where we lay on the bed, made love, and talked for a long time in the dark. I was contented enough, but there was always a part of myself, warm and alive, that longed for tears, solitude, and excitement. I thought perhaps my liver was out of order.

The Friday before going to lunch at Luc's I called to see Catherine for half an hour. She was vivacious, domineering, and always in love. I accepted rather than chose her friendship. She looked upon me as a fragile, defenceless girl, which pleased me, and I often thought her wonderful. In her eyes my indifference gave me a certain aura, as it had to Bertrand until a sudden desire to possess me got hold of him.

Just then she was infatuated with a cousin and told me a long idyllic story about him. I said I was lunching with relations of Bertrand's, and suddenly realized I had rather forgotten Luc and I regretted it. Why couldn't I recount one of those interminable love stories to amuse her? But she did not expect it. We were used to our respective roles: she talked, I listened; she gave advice and I ceased to listen.

This visit depressed me. I arrived at Luc's house without enthusiasm and in rather a panic. I would have to be polite and entertaining, and try to create a good impression, whereas I should have preferred to lunch alone, twirl a mustard-pot round in my fingers, and gaze vaguely at nothing.

Bertrand was already there, alone with Luc's wife. I saw a beautiful face which made me think of a full-blown rose. She was blonde, tall, and rather heavily built; in fact lovely, but not in a striking way. She seemed to me the type of woman whom many men would like to have to keep, one who would make them happy, a sweet woman. Was I sweet? I would ask Bertrand. I certainly held his hand and talked softly and stroked his hair. But I hated talking loudly, and I liked to smooth his hair, which felt firm and warm, like an animal's fur.

Françoise put me at ease at once. She showed me over their luxurious apartment, and settled me in an armchair with a drink. I was quite charmed with her. The embarrassment I had felt because of my old skirt and shabby sweater soon passed. Luc was expected, but was still at work. Perhaps I ought to assume some interest in his profession, which I had never thought of doing. The questions I would have liked to ask people were: 'Are you in love? What are you reading?' But I never bothered about anyone's work, thought it is often of primary importance to them.

'You look worried,' Françoise said, laughingly. 'Would you like some more whisky?'

'Yes, please,' I said.

'Dominique already has the reputation of being a drunkard,' said Bertrand; 'do you know why?'

He jumped up and came over to me with an air of importance.

'Her upper lip is rather short, and when she closes her eyes to drink it gives her a look of fanaticism.'

While speaking he had taken my upper lip between his thumb and index finger. He showed me to Françoise as if I were a puppy.

I began to laugh and he let me go. Luc came in.

When I saw him I thought again how handsome he was, but this time with a sort of pang. It really hurt me to like something I could not have. I seldom wanted anything, but just then I knew that I would have liked to grasp his face in my hands, squeeze it violently between my fingers and press his full mouth against mine. Yet Luc was not really handsome. I was to hear that repeated many times afterwards, but though I had only seen him twice, there was something about his features which made his face seem a thousand times more familiar to me than Bertrand's. A thousand times less strange and a thousand times more desirable than Bertrand's, which all the same I liked.

Luc greeted us and sat down. He could be astonishingly immobile. He had something very tense in the slowness of his movements, the relaxation of his body, that made me uneasy. He looked fondly at Françoise. I looked at him. I do not remember now what we said. The conversation was mainly between Bertrand and Françoise. I cannot bear to think of those preliminaries. If at that moment I had been a little more careful to keep away from him, I could still have escaped. But now, on the contrary, I can hardly wait until I come to the first time he made me happy. Even the thought of describing my feelings fills me with a bitter, impatient joy.

We went out after lunch. In the street I immediately walked in step with Luc's rapid stride and forgot Bertrand's. Luc took my elbow to help me across the road, which embarrassed me. I did not know what to do with my forearm, nor with my hand which hung down disconsolately as though my arm had gone dead below the part he held. I did not remember how I managed with Bertrand. Later Luc and Françoise took me to a dressmaker and bought me a rust-coloured coat. In my bewilderment I hardly knew whether to refuse it or to thank them. Already there was something that seemed to race like a hurricane when Luc was there. Afterwards time suddenly dropped back to normal, and once more there were minutes, hours, and cigarettes.

Bertrand was furious with me for accepting the coat. After we left he made a violent scene.

'It's simply incredible! I suppose you'd just take anything anyone offered you!'

'It's not anyone, it's your uncle,' I said hypocritically. 'In any case, I couldn't have afforded that coat myself, it's frightfully expensive.'

'You could have done without it, I imagine?'

During the past two hours I had grown accustomed to wearing the coat, which suited me perfectly, and I was shocked by his last words. Bertrand could not understand my kind of logic and we quarrelled. In the end he took me to his room without any dinner, as if to a punishment; a 'punishment' which for him, as

I well knew, was the most essential and important part of his whole day.

He trembled as he kissed me, with a respect which both touched and frightened me. How much I had preferred the carefree gaiety of our first embraces. But now, when I felt his impatience, I forgot everything and only he and I existed. It was the Bertrand I knew so well in the pleasure and agony of love. Even today, perhaps more than ever today, that pleasure seems a priceless present, and however one may mock at it, or try to reason about it, I still call it the essence of love.

3

There were frequent dinners, either just the four of us or with some of Luc's friends. Then Françoise went away for ten days. I loved her already. She was unfailingly kind and generous to people, and yet at moments was afraid of not understanding them, and this charmed me more than anything. She was like the earth, reassuring like the earth, and sometimes childlike. When they were together, she and Luc were very gay.

We saw her off at the Gare de Lyon. I was less shy than at first, almost natural, in fact in very good spirits. For with the complete disappearance of my boredom, to which I had not dared to give a name, I had changed for the better. I became lively and even amusing; it seemed to me that this state of things could go on for ever. I had grown used to Luc's face, and attributed the sudden emotion I sometimes felt at the sight of it to an aesthetic pleasure, or to affection.

At the door of the railway carriage Françoise smiled as she said:

'I leave him in your care.'

On the way back Bertrand stopped to buy a political journal, which would give him an excuse to get annoyed. All at once Luc turned to me and said very quickly:

'Shall we have dinner together tomorrow?'

I was about to reply; 'All right, I'll tell Bertrand,' when he cut me short: 'I'll ring you up,' and to Bertrand who came back at that moment he said: 'Which paper have you bought?'

'I couldn't get the one I wanted,' said Bertrand. 'Dominique, we have a lecture. I think we'll have to hurry.'

He had taken my arm and continued to hold it. Bertrand and Luc eyed each other with mutual suspicion. I felt disconcerted. With Françoise gone, everything became confused and unpleasant, and Luc's first sign of interest in me remains a painful memory, for I realized I had been deliberately shutting my eyes to the truth. I badly wanted Françoise back as a protector. I realized that our quartet had existed on a false basis, for like all those who easily tell lies, I was responsive to atmosphere and sincere in playing the role I chose.

'I'll take you to the Sorbonne,' said Luc casually. He had a fast open car which he drove well. On the way we said nothing except 'See you soon' as we got out.

'As a matter of fact, I'm rather relieved Françoise has gone away,' said Bertrand; 'one can't always see the same people.'

I understood he was shutting Luc out of our future plans, but I was becoming careful, and kept quiet.

'And besides,' Bertrand went on, 'they're rather old for us, aren't they?'

I did not reply and we went in to Breme's philosophy lecture. I sat perfectly still and listened. So Luc wanted to have dinner alone with me. That was probably what happiness meant. I spread out my fingers on the wooden bench, and felt an irrepressible little smile lifting the corner of my mouth. I turned away so that Bertrand would not notice. It lasted only a moment, then I said to myself, 'you're making too much of the whole thing; it's all quite normal really. You must burn your boats, not think of the consequences, and not let yourself be taken in'; these were my natural youthful reactions.

The next day I made up my mind to treat the dinner with Luc as a frivolous adventure. I imagined his rushing in and eagerly making me a declaration. In fact, he came rather late, looking absent-minded, and my one wish was that he would show some sign of agitation at our impromptu meeting. He did nothing of the sort, but talked easily about one thing and another, so that in the end I found myself following his lead. He was probably the first person with whom I had ever felt completely at ease with no mental reservations. Afterwards he suggested our going to a restaurant to dance, and took me to Sonny's. There he met friends who joined us, and I thought what a vain idiot I had been to imagine for a moment that he would have wanted to be alone with me.

When I looked round at the women at our table I realized that I was neither elegant nor witty. On the contrary, towards midnight there remained nothing of the vamp I had all day imagined myself to be, but a prostrate rag of a girl, ashamed of her dress, and longing for Bertrand, who at least thought her pretty.

Luc's friends were talking of the benefit of Alka-seltzer the morning after a party. I realized there were many people who took Alka-seltzer, and treated their bodies like precious playthings to use for their amusement and nurse with care. Perhaps I ought to abandon my books, serious conversations, long walks, and give myself over to the pleasures money can buy; to futile talk and other absorbing distractions. The thing was to possess the means to beautify myself. Did Luc care for these women, I wondered.

He turned to me, smiling, and asked me to dance. He took me in his arms, gently placed my head against his chin, and we danced. I was very conscious of his body close to mine.

'All these people bore you, don't they?' he said. 'The women do nothing but twitter.'

'I've never been to a real night-club,' I said; 'I'm dazzled.'

He began to laugh:

'How strange you are, Dominique. You amuse me. Let's go on somewhere else and talk.'

We left Sonny's. Luc took me to a bar and we began to drink deliberately. Besides liking whisky, I knew that I could only talk freely when I was a little drunk. I soon saw Luc as an agreeable and charming person, and no longer terrifying, and even felt a great tenderness for him.

Naturally we began to talk about love. He told me that it was a very good thing, less important than people made out, but that there must be a lot of love on both sides in order to be happy. I nodded. He said that he was happy because he and Françoise loved each other very much. I congratulated him, and assured him that I was not at all surprised because he and Françoise were very, very nice people. I was becoming more and more emotional.

'By the way,' said Luc, 'I would very much like to make love to you.'

I began to laugh stupidly. I felt incapable of any reaction. 'And Françoise?' I said.

'Perhaps I'll tell her. She's very fond of you, you know.'

'That's just it,' I said, 'but somehow one doesn't talk about things like that.'

I felt indignant, but my constant change from one state of mind to another was beginning to wear me out. It seemed to me both extremely natural and extremely improper that Luc wanted to sleep with me.

'In a way,' said Luc seriously, 'there is something; I mean between us. God knows I don't usually care for young girls. But we're very alike, you know. What I mean is that it wouldn't seem either silly or banal, and that is a rare thing. Well, you think it over.'

'That's it,' I said, 'I'll think it over.'

I must have been in a pitiable state. Luc leaned across and kissed my cheek.

'Poor darling,' he said, 'I'm so sorry for you. If you only had some elementary notion of morals. But you haven't, any more than I have. And you're nice, and you're fond of Françoise, and you're less bored with me than with Bertrand. That's you!'

He burst out laughing. I was annoyed. After that I always felt rather exasperated when Luc began, as he called it, to sum up the situation. Just then I couldn't help showing it.

'It doesn't matter,' he said. 'Nothing is really important in that sort of thing. I am very fond of you, I care for you, we'll have a lot of fun together, just fun.'

'I hate you!' I said.

I made my voice sound very gloomy and we both began to laugh. The complicity we had established during the past three minutes struck me as a bit dubious.

'Now I'm going to take you home,' said Luc. 'It's very late. Or if you like we'll go to the Quai de Bercy to see the sunrise.'

We went to the Quai de Bercy. Luc stopped the car. The sky was white above the Seine, which lay between the cranes like a sad child between its toys. The sky was both white and grey. It rose towards the day above the dead houses, the bridges and railway lines, slowly, indomitably, as it did every morning. Next to me Luc smoked in silence. His profile was immobile. I held out my hand, he took it, and we went slowly back towards the pension. In front of the door he let go my hand. I got out and we smiled at each other. I collapsed on to my bed, and with the thought that I ought to undress, wash my stockings, and hang up my dress, I fell asleep.

4

I awoke with a painful sensation of having an urgent problem to solve. For what Luc proposed was in fact a game – an alluring game – but one which would destroy a real feeling I had for Bertrand, and also something confused within myself, something complicated and bitter: for even though I might sometimes feel that all passion and all love affairs are short-lived, I was not prepared to accept this as a necessity, especially when it was imposed upon me by Luc. Like all those who look upon life as a comedy, I could not bear to perform in one that I had not written myself.

I knew quite well that when this game was played between two people who were really attracted to each other, as a temporary solution for their loneliness, it was bound to be dangerous. It was foolish to pretend to be stronger than I was. From the moment when Luc would have 'tamed me' (as Françoise put it), and openly acknowledged me, I would be unable to leave him without suffering. Bertrand was not capable of giving me anything more than love, though I say that with affection, but where Luc was concerned, I made no such reservations. For anyhow, when one is young, nothing seems more exquisitely desirable than to take risks. I had never, so far, decided anything for myself, the choice had always been made for me. Why, this time, should I offer any resistance? There would be Luc's charm, the days to be got through, and then the evenings with him. It would all come about quite naturally; it was useless to try to see into the future.

With this blissful solution to my problems I went to the Sorbonne, where I met Bertrand and other friends and we had lunch in the Rue Cujas, and although this was a daily occurrence, that day it seemed abnormal to me. My real place was with Luc. I was puzzling it all out while Jean-Jacques, a friend of Bertrand's, made sarcastic remarks about my faraway look.

'I can't understand it, Dominique. You must be in love! Bertrand, what have you done to this absent-minded young woman, turned her into a Princesse de Clèves?'

'I don't know what you're talking about,' said Bertrand.

I looked at him. He was red in the face and avoided my glance. It was unbelievable that my friend and companion for the past year had suddenly become an adversary. I made a movement towards him. I would have liked to remind him of our summer days, our winter days, and his room, and to add that all this couldn't be wiped out in three weeks, it wasn't possible. And I would have liked him to agree vehemently with me, to reassure me, and to take me back because he loved me. But he was not a man. With certain men, amongst them Luc, one discerned a hidden strength that neither Bertrand nor any of the other very young men I knew possessed.

'Leave Dominique alone!' said Catherine in her usual dictatorial way. 'Come with me, Dominique, men are brutes; let's go and have coffee together.'

Outside she explained that I mustn't take Bertrand's attitude too seriously, for he was very attached to me, and I mustn't worry about his little fits of bad temper. I did not protest. After all, it was better for Bertrand not to be humiliated before our friends. As for me, I was sick of their speeches, their gossip, their infantile flirtations, and their tragedies, but all the same, Bertrand's suffering must be considered, and I could not ignore it. It would all happen so quickly. So far there was only a small rift between Bertrand and myself, but I knew they would begin talking about us, analysing the situation, and annoying me to such an extent that it might become a definite break.

'You don't understand,' I said to Catherine; 'it's not a question of Bertrand.'

'Ah!' she said.

I turned towards her and saw such curiosity, such a mania for interfering, and such a vampire-like expression on her face, that I began to laugh. 'I'm thinking of going into a convent,' I said gravely.

Without showing any surprise, Catherine started off on a long monologue about the pleasures of life, the little birds, the sun, etc. . . . 'all that you would be giving up for this madness.' She also spoke about more sensual pleasures, lowering her voice and whispering: 'it's just as well to talk about these things, after all, they're important!' If I had really meant what I said, she would certainly have succeeded in precipitating me into the arms of the Church by her description of the pleasures of life. Was it really possible that people only lived for 'that'? Anyhow, if I were bored, at least I was passionately bored. Besides, Catherine showed herself to be so familiar with low haunts, so anxious for promiscuous adventures, so ready with odious detailed confidences, that I was thankful to leave her standing on the pavement. Humming gaily as I walked away, I thought: 'Let's get rid of Catherine and all her attachments too!'

I wandered about for an hour, went into a lot of shops, and talked to everyone. I felt absolutely light-hearted. Paris belonged to me: Paris belonged to the unscrupulous, to the irresponsible; I had always felt it, but it had hurt because I was not carefree enough. Now it was my city, my beautiful, shining, golden city, 'the city that stands aloof'. I was carried along by something that must have been joy. I walked quickly, was full of impatience, and could feel the blood coursing through my veins. I felt ridiculously young at those moments of mad happiness and much nearer to reality and truth than when I searched my soul in my moods of sadness.

I went into a cinema in the Champs-Élysées where they showed old films. A young man came and sat down beside me. A glance showed me that he was good-looking, perhaps a little too fair. Soon he touched my elbow with his, put a hand out discreetly towards my knee: I caught it and kept it in mine. I wanted to laugh and giggle like a schoolgirl. Was this the notorious promiscuity of dark corners, the furtive, shameless embrace? I was holding the warm hand of an unknown young man in mine, although I had no use for him, and it amused me. He stroked my hand; slowly advanced one knee. I submitted with a sort of curiosity, fear, and encouragement. Like him, I was half afraid that my sense of dignity would suddenly awake, and that I would behave like an old lady who leaves her seat in disgust. My heart was beating a little fast: was it emotion or the film? The film was good, by the way. There ought to be a special place where old films are shown to people who need a friend. The young man turned a questioning face to me, and because the film was very bright, I saw that he was really rather handsome. 'Yes, but not my type,' I said to myself as his face came slowly closer to mine. I thought for a moment that the people behind us must be wondering . . . he kissed well, but at the same time his hand tightened on my knee and advanced slyly, stupidly trying to gain a further advantage which so far I had not refused. I got up and went out. He must have wondered why.

I was back in the Champs-Élysées with the taste of a strange mouth on my lips, and I decided to go home and read a new novel.

It was a beautiful book by Sartre, *L'Âge de Raison*. I threw myself into it with pleasure. I was young, I liked one man and another was in love with me. I had one of those silly little girlish problems to solve. I was feeling rather important. There was even a married man involved, and another woman: a little play with four characters was taking place in the springtime in Paris. I reduced it all to a lovely dry equation, as cynical as could be. Besides, I felt remarkably sure of myself. I accepted all the unhappiness, the conflict, the pleasure to come; I mockingly accepted it all in advance.

I read on, while it gradually got dark, I put my book down, leaned my head on my arm and watched the sky turn from mauve to grey. I suddenly felt weak and helpless. My life was slipping away, and I did nothing except sneer. If only there were someone close to my cheek, whom I could keep there, whom I could press against me with love's agonized violence. I was not cynical enough to envy Bertrand, but sad enough to envy all happy lovers, all desperate meetings, all slavery. I got up and went out.

5

I went out several times with Luc during the two following weeks, but his friends always came too. They were, generally, travellers with entertaining stories to tell. Luc talked quickly, was amusing, and looked at me affectionately, but he always seemed distracted and pressed for time, which made me doubt whether he was really interested in me. Afterwards he drove me to my door, got out of the car, and kissed me lightly on the cheek before leaving. I was both relieved and disappointed that he no longer spoke of the desire he had said he felt for me. Finally, he announced that Françoise was returning next day, and I realized that the last two weeks had passed like a dream and I had been worrying a great deal about nothing.

We went to fetch Françoise from the station, but without Bertrand, who for the last ten days had been sulking. I was sorry for him, but took advantage of it to lead an aimless, lazy life, on my own, which suited me. I knew it made him unhappy not to see me and that prevented me being really happy myself.

Françoise arrived one morning, all smiles, kissed us, and declared that we did not look at all well, and that it couldn't have happened at a better moment, for we were invited to spend the week-end with Luc's sister, Bertrand's mother. I protested that I was not invited and had had a slight quarrel with Bertrand. Luc added that his sister exasperated him. But Françoise arranged everything. Bertrand had asked his mother to invite me, Françoise said, probably to make up this ridiculous quarrel, and as for Luc, he occasionally had to show some family feeling.

She looked laughingly at me and I smiled at her, full of good-will. She had grown fatter, but was so warm-hearted, so trusting that I was delighted to think that nothing had happened between Luc and me and we could all three be happy together as before. We had been sensible, Luc and I. Yet as I got into the car to sit between him and Françoise I glanced at him for a second and the thought that I was renouncing him gave me a strange, disagreeable little shock. All the same I quite looked forward to seeing Bertrand again.

On a lovely evening we drove down to Bertrand's mother. I knew that when her husband died he had left her a nice country house, and the idea of going to spend a week-end somewhere satisfied a certain snobbishness in me that I hadn't had an opportunity of indulging until then. Bertrand had told me that his mother was a very charming woman. He said it in the detached way some young people assume when talking of their parents, to emphasize that their real life is elsewhere. I had gone to the expense of buying a pair of linen slacks, Catherine's being really too big for me. This purchase had exceeded my allowance, but I knew that Luc and Françoise would provide for my needs if necessary. I was astonished by my willingness to accept gifts from them, but like most people who are inclined to be indulgent towards themselves, I attributed this tendency more to their generosity than to my own weakness. It is easier to admire others than to find fault with oneself.

Luc had come with Françoise to fetch us from a café on the Boulevard Saint-Michel. He was again looking tired and rather sad. On the open road he began to drive very fast and danger-ously. Fear made Bertrand burst out laughing, and I joined in. Françoise turned round on hearing us laugh. She had the defeated look of amiable people who never dare to protest, even to protect their very lives.

'What are you laughing at?'

'They are young,' said Luc. 'Twenty is the age of hilarious laughter.'

I don't know why this phrase irritated me. I didn't like Luc to treat Bertrand and me like a couple, especially like a couple of children.

'It's nervous laughter,' I said, 'because you drive too fast and we are frightened.'

'You must come with me,' said Luc, 'and I'll teach you to drive.' It was the first time that he had used the word 'tu' to me in public. Perhaps it was only a tactless blunder. Françoise looked at Luc for a second. Then I changed my mind about it being a blunder. I didn't believe in revealing slips of the tongue, intercepted glances, and swift intuitions. There was a phrase that always surprised me in novels: 'And suddenly she knew that he lied.'

Anyhow, we were now arriving. Luc turned sharply down a little lane and I was thrown against Bertrand. He held me against him solidly, tenderly, and I felt very embarrassed. I couldn't stand Luc seeing me like that. It seemed vulgar, and rather stupid, even somewhat indelicate.

'You look like a bird,' said Françoise.

She had turned round to us. It was really a friendly look. She had not the air of an accomplice, of the mature woman who is a party to an adolescent romance. Her glance simply implied that I looked nice in Bertrand's arms and rather touching. I liked the idea of looking touching. It has often saved me from believing, thinking, or answering.

'An old bird,' I said, 'I feel quite old.'

'I do too,' said Françoise, 'but with more reason.'

Luc turned his head towards her with a little smile. I thought suddenly 'they like each other'. I expect they still make love quite often. Luc sleeps next to her, lies next to her, loves her – I wonder what he thinks about Bertrand and me. Is he in fact as jealous of him as I am of Françoise?

'Ah, here we are at the house,' said Bertrand. 'There's another car and I'm afraid my mother has some of her usual guests.'

'In that case we'll leave,' said Luc. 'I've a horror of my dear sister's friends. I know a charming little inn quite near.'

'Come along,' said Françoise, 'we've had enough grumbling. In any case, this house is charming, and Dominique doesn't know it yet. Come, Dominique.'

She took me by the hand and led me towards a rather pretty house surrounded by lawns. I thought to myself that I had just missed doing her a bad turn by deceiving her with Luc, and that I liked her very much and would hate to cause her pain, though in any case she wouldn't have known.

'Here you are at last,' said a high-pitched voice. Bertrand's mother emerged from a gap in the hedge. I had never met her. She threw me a searching glance such as mothers of young men often inflict on young girls their sons introduce to them. She seemed to be particularly blonde and flashy, and immediately started twittering round us in an exasperating way. Luc looked upon her as a calamity. Bertrand was obviously a little uncomfortable, which forced me to be specially gracious. Finally, I was relieved to find myself in my bedroom. The bed was very high with coarse sheets like the beds I had been used to in my childhood. I opened the window, which looked out on green rustling trees, and a strong smell of wet earth and grass permeated the room.

'Do you like it?' asked Bertrand.

He looked both confused and pleased and I thought that for him this week-end with me at his mother's must mean something rather important and complicated. I smiled at him.

'You've a very nice house. As for your mother, I don't know her, but she seems charming.'

Françoise Sagan

'So you're pleased you came? By the way, I've got the room next to yours.'

He laughed like an accomplice and I joined in. I like strange houses and bathrooms with black and white tiles, large windows, and domineering young men. He took me in his arms and kissed me gently on the mouth. I knew his breath, his manner of kissing, and I had never told him of the young man at the cinema. He would have taken it badly. I also took it badly now. Looking back, I had a rather shameful memory of it, both comical and uneasy; altogether unpleasant. I had been in a strange mood that afternoon. I wasn't so any more.

'Come and have dinner,' I said to Bertrand, who was leaning over to kiss me again, his eyes a little dilated. I liked him to desire me. On the other hand, I didn't like myself very much.

The dinner was a deadly bore. There were, in fact, some friends of Bertrand's mother, a common-place couple. When dessert came round, the husband, who was called Richard and was chairman of some public company, made the usual remark of his generation.

'Well, young lady, are you one of these unhappy existential-ists? As a matter of fact, my dear Marthe' – he was talking to Bertrand's mother – 'these disillusioned young people are beyond me. At their age, dash it, one loved life. In my time one enjoyed oneself. One went off the deep end occasionally, but at least it was amusing!'

His wife and Bertrand's mother laughed in an understanding way. Luc yawned. Bertrand prepared an answer which no one would listen to. With her natural good humour Françoise busily tried to understand why they were so boring. As for me, it was not the first time that gentlemen with pink cheeks and grey hair had aimed their healthy humour at me while masticating their food. What added piquancy to their talk was that they hadn't the faintest idea of the real meaning of the word 'existentialism'. I made no reply.

'My dear Richard,' said Luc, 'at your age, at our age I mean, I'm afraid the gay life is over. These young people make love, which is only right. One needs a girl secretary in an office to be gay.'

The gay dog did not answer. The rest of dinner passed quietly; everybody talked except Luc and myself. He was the only one who was as bored as I was, and I wondered if the incapacity to stand up to boredom was not one of the chief things we had in common.

After dinner we went on to the terrace as the weather was mild. Bertrand left us to find some whisky. Luc came over to me and told me in a low voice not to drink too much.

'At any rate, I'm behaving myself,' I said, vexed.

'I would be jealous,' he said, 'I would only want you to drink too much and say stupid things with me.'

'And the rest of the time what would I do?'

'Pull a long face as at dinner.'

'And you,' I said, 'do you think your face was gay? You don't seem to believe in the "good old times" in spite of the way you were talking.'

He laughed. 'Come and have a walk with me in the garden?'

'In the dark? What about Bertrand and the others?' I was in a panic.

'Oh, they've bored us enough. Come on, let's go.'

He took me by the arm, turning his back on the others. Bertrand hadn't yet arrived with the whisky. I thought vaguely that on his return he would rush out and try to find us under a tree and probably kill Luc as in *Pelléas et Mélisande*.

'I am taking this young girl for a stroll,' he called to them.

I didn't turn round, but heard Françoise laugh. Luc led me down a gravel path which seemed white to start with but drifted into darkness. I was suddenly very frightened. I felt I wanted to be with my parents by the River Yonne.

'I am frightened,' I said to Luc.

He didn't laugh, but took hold of my hand. I would have wished him to be always like this, silent, a little grave, protective, and tender, to say he loved me, and to take me in his arms. He stopped, and took me in his arms. I was against his suit with my eyes closed. All the previous period had been a long escape until this very moment; his hands lifting my face, and his mouth, sweet and just made for mine. He kept his fingers round my face and held me tightly with them while we kissed. I put my arms round his neck. I was young and frightened of myself, of him, and of everything that was not the present moment. I immediately adored his mouth.

Luc didn't say a word, but kissed me, lifting his head now and then to regain his breath. I saw his face above mine in the semi-darkness like a mask, distracted and concentrated at the same time. I shut my eyes under the heat which enveloped my eyelids, my temples and throat. Something happened to me that I didn't understand, which had neither the haste nor impatience of desire, but something that was happy, slow, and thrilling.

Luc detached himself from me and I stumbled a little. He took me by the arm and we went round the garden without saying a word. I said to myself that I would like to go on kissing him until daybreak without another gesture. Bertrand so quickly exhausted his kissing. Desire rendered it useless in his eyes. It was only a step towards pleasure, instead of something lasting and sufficient in itself, as Luc made me feel it.

'Your garden is lovely,' said Luc, smiling at his sister.

'Unfortunately it is rather late.'

'It is never too late,' said Bertrand testily. He looked at me. I turned my eyes away. What I wanted was to be alone in the darkness, to be able to recall and understand those few moments in the park. I would put my thoughts aside while the conversation was going on. Then later I would be up in my room with this memory. I would lie flat on my bed with my eyes wide open, would picture it all before me, and either destroy it or let it become something essential. That night I locked my door, but Bertrand did not try to come in.

6

The morning passed slowly. Awakening had been enjoyable, like an awakening in childhood. It was not like one of those long, dreary, and solitary days – broken up by books and study; it was the other kind. By the other kind I mean days in which I had a part to play, in which I had to take responsibility. The thought of this responsibility overwhelmed me at first, and I pressed my head into my pillow, with a feeling of physical discomfort. Then I remembered the previous evening, and Luc's kisses, and something very tender stirred my heart.

The bathroom was most luxurious. Once in the bath I began to sing to a gay jazz tune the words 'And now, and now, I must make a decision.' Someone knocked on the wall. It was Luc.

'Aren't honest folk allowed to sleep?'

He had a happy voice. Had I been born six years earlier, before Françoise, we might have lived together and he would have laughingly prevented me singing in the early morning. We would have slept together. We would have been happy for a long time, whilst now we found ourselves in a quandary. It was a real quandary, and that is why we dared not risk getting more deeply involved, in spite of our pretence of bored indifference. I ought to escape, to go away. I got out of my bath, but putting on a fluffy bath-towel, which smelt of old country cupboards, I said to myself that the sensible thing to do was to let things run their course and not to worry. It wasn't any good trying to analyse, I just had to wait and see.

I tried on the slacks that I had bought and glanced at myself in the looking-glass. I didn't altogether care for my appearance. My hair was untidy, but my face was pointed and had a sweet expression. I wished that I had regular features and long hair and looked romantic and sensual. These trousers were ridiculous, too narrow, and I'd never dare go down in them. It was a form of despair that I knew only too well, when I disliked my appearance so much that I would feel miserable if I decided to go out.

And then Françoise knocked, came in, and put everything right.

'My dear little Dominique, how charming you look like that! You seem even younger and more attractive than usual. You put me to shame.'

She was sitting on the bed and looking at herself in the mirror.

'I eat too many cakes because I can't resist them, and I have wrinkles too!'

She did have rather deep wrinkles round her eyes. I touched them.

'I think wrinkles are wonderful,' I said lovingly. 'Imagine all the nights, all the countries, all the faces that have gone to make even those two tiny lines. They improve you, they make you look more alive. And in any case I think they're beautiful, expressive, moving. I have a horror of smooth faces.'

She burst out laughing.

'I believe you'd ruin every beauty parlour so as to console me. You're really sweet, Dominique, very sweet.'

I was ashamed.

'I'm not as sweet as all that.'

'Do I annoy you? Young people hate to be thought sweet. But you never say anything disagreeable or unjust. And you like people. So I think you're perfect.'

'I am not.'

It was a long time since I had talked about myself. It was a game I enjoyed when I was seventeen, but now I was tired of it. In fact, only if Luc were to be interested in me or cared for me would I take an interest in myself, or care for myself, but this was a stupid thought.

'I'm exaggerating,' I said aloud.

'And you're incredibly absent-minded,' said Françoise.

'Because I'm not in love,' I said.

She looked at me, and I was very tempted to say to her, 'Françoise, I am falling in love with Luc, but I'm also very fond of you. Please take him away.'

'What about Bertrand, is it really over?'

I shrugged my shoulders.

'I don't see him any more. I mean I don't look at him any more.'

'You ought perhaps to tell him?'

I did not reply. Why should I say to Bertrand, 'I don't want to see you any more,' when I didn't mind seeing him and was fond of him? Françoise smiled.

'I understand, it isn't as easy as all that. Come and have lunch. In the Rue Caumartin I saw a lovely jersey which would go beautifully with your trousers. We'll go and look at it together and . . .'

We talked gaily of clothes and walked down the stairs. The subject did not interest me very much, but I liked to talk like that to suggest a wrong adjective, make a mistake so that she could correct me, and laugh. Downstairs, Luc and Bertrand were having lunch. They were talking of bathing.

'We might go to the swimming-pool,' Bertrand was saying. He must have thought that he could face the sunshine better than Luc. But perhaps I was mistaken.

'It's an excellent idea, and on the way I might teach Dominique how to drive.'

'No foolishness. No foolishness,' said Bertrand's mother, who came into the room draped in a sumptuous dressing-gown. 'Have you all slept well? And you, my little one?'

Bertrand looked uncomfortable. He put on a dignified expression which did not suit him. I preferred him to be gay. One likes people one is hurting to be gay. It is less upsetting.

Luc got up. He obviously could not stand his sister's presence. It made me laugh. At times I have also had these physical aversions but have been obliged to hide them. There was something childish about Luc.

'I'm going to fetch my bathing things.'

There was a scramble, everyone trying to find their things. Finally, when we were all ready, Bertrand went with his mother in their friend's car, and we three were left together.

'You drive,' said Luc.

I had some vague notions of driving and it did not work out too badly. Luc sat next to me, and Françoise, unconscious of the danger, talked from her seat in the back. I had a violent nostalgia for what might have been. Long journeys with Luc beside me, the car lights illuminating the white road at night, myself leaning on Luc's shoulder. Luc solidly at the wheel, driving too fast, the dawn on the countryside, sunsets over the sea . . .

'You know, I've never seen the sea.'

It was a surprise.

'I'll take you there,' said Luc softly, and turning towards me he smiled. It was like a promise. Françoise had not heard it and said:

'Next time we go to the sea, Luc, we must take her. She'll say, "Oh! what a lot of water! I love it!"'

'I'd probably bathe first,' I said, 'and talk about it later.'

'You know it's really lovely,' said Françoise. 'The beaches are yellow, with red rocks and all that blue sea that sweeps over them . . .'

'I adore your descriptions,' said Luc, laughing, 'yellow, blue, and red – like a schoolgirl – a young schoolgirl, of course,' he added apologetically, turning towards me. 'There are old schoolgirls, very very clever indeed. Turn right, Dominique, if you can.'

I could. We arrived in front of a lawn. In the middle of the lawn was a large swimming-pool full of blue water, the sight of which made me freeze.

We soon assembled round the pool in our bathing-suits. I met Luc coming out of his cabin and looking annoyed. When I asked him why, he said with a worried smile:

'I'm afraid I'm not very handsome.'

He wasn't. He was tall and thin, a little bent and not sunburnt. He seemed unhappy, he held his towel in front of him very carefully.

'Come, on!' I said jokingly. 'You're not as ugly as all that.'

He gave me a sidelong glance and burst out laughing.

'Young woman, you are beginning to be disrespectful.'

He plunged into the water, but came out quickly with cries of distress. Françoise sat on the side of the pool. I thought her more attractive than when she was dressed. She looked like one of the statues at the Louvre.

'It's terribly cold,' said Luc. 'One must be mad to bathe in May.'

'In April don't take off a stitch – in May do as you please,' said Bertrand's mother pompously.

But as soon as she had touched the water with her toe she went off to get dressed. I looked round the pool at our gay little group. I felt it was a pleasant occasion, but as usual could not help saying to myself: 'What are you doing here?'

'Are you going to bathe?' said Bertrand.

He stood before me on one foot and I looked at him approvingly. I knew he did dumb-bell exercises each morning. We had once spent a week-end together and, thinking I was still asleep, he had performed various exercises in front of the window – exercises that had made me laugh until I nearly cried. He had a clean, healthy look about him.

'We're lucky to have dark skins,' he said, looking at the others.

'Come on, let us get into the water,' I said. I was afraid he would begin making unpleasant remarks about his mother, who exasperated him.

I jumped into the water very reluctantly, swam round the pool so as not to be beaten, and came up with my teeth chattering. Françoise rubbed me down with a towel. I was wondering why she never had any children. She was so obviously made for motherhood, with her broad hips, well-developed body and her gentleness. It was a pity.

7

I had arranged to meet Luc at six o'clock two days after that week-end. It seemed that now there was something irrevocable between us. It was no longer possible to be merely frivolous. I wished I were a seventeenth-century girl and could ask for reparation for a kiss.

We were to meet at the bar in the Quai Voltaire. To my surprise, when I arrived, Luc was already there. He did not look at all well and seemed tired. I sat next to him and he immediately ordered two whiskies. Then he asked me for news of Bertrand.

'He's well.'

'Is he suffering?' He did not ask in a sarcastic tone, but very quietly.

'Why should he suffer?'

'He's not a fool.'

'I don't know why you should talk about Bertrand. It's . . . well . . .'

'Secondary.' He said this ironically, which maddened me.

'It's not secondary, but neither is it very important. Talking of something important, let's rather discuss Françoise.'

He burst out laughing:

'It's funny, but in this kind of situation, the partner of the other always seems a more serious obstacle than one's own. It seems a dreadful thing to say, but when you know somebody, you also know the way they suffer, and it seems more bearable. I say "bearable", but I would rather say "known", and therefore less frightening.'

'I don't know Bertrand's capacity for suffering,' I said.

'You haven't had time. I've been married for ten years, and have seen Françoise suffer. It is very disagreeable.'

For a moment we both remained quite still, probably imagining Françoise suffering. In my mind's eye I saw Françoise with her face to the wall.

'It's foolish,' said Luc at last. 'But you understand, it is not so simple as I thought.'

He took up his whisky, threw back his head, and swallowed it. It was like being at the cinema. I tried to persuade myself that this was no time to be out of touch with reality, yet everything seemed unreal to me. Luc was there, he would decide, everything was going to be all right.

He leaned forward a little, holding his empty glass and swirling the ice round and round in it. He spoke without looking at me:

'I've had affairs, naturally. Françoise mostly did not know about them except on a few unfortunate occasions. But they were never serious.' He straightened himself up in a kind of rage: 'It's not very serious for you either, but what about Françoise?'

I listened without suffering. I do not know why, but I seemed to be at a lecture on philosophy which had no reference to myself.

'But this time it is different. At the beginning I wanted you, as a man of my kind can desire a little, feline, difficult, self-willed girl. As I've already told you, I wanted to possess you, to spend a night with you. I never thought . . .'

Suddenly he turned towards me, took my hands, and spoke gently. I looked closely at his face and marked every detail. I listened with passionate attention to his words, and I forgot about myself and my little inner voice.

'I never thought I would come to admire you. I do very much, Dominique. I love you very much. I can't promise to love you for "ever and ever" as children say, but we are very alike, you know. I not only want to sleep with you, I want to live with you, go away with you on a holiday. We would be very happy, very loving, I would show you the sea, teach you about money, and how to feel more free. We'd be less bored, that's all.'

'I would like that too,' I said.

'Afterwards I'd go back to Françoise. What do you risk? To get attached to me? To suffer afterwards? But after all, that's better than being bored. You'd rather be happy and even unhappy than nothing at all, wouldn't you?'

'Obviously,' I replied.

'Isn't it true that you'd risk nothing?' repeated Luc, as if to convince himself.

'Why talk about suffering?' I said. 'One must not exaggerate. I'm not so tender-hearted.'

'Good,' said Luc. 'We shall see. We'll think it over. Let's talk of something else. Would you like another drink?'

We drank each other's health. Uppermost in my mind was that we should probably go away together in a car, as I had imagined and thought impossible. And I would take care not to get too attached to him. Knowing that the boats were burned in advance, I wasn't going to be so foolish.

Afterwards we walked along the quay. Luc laughed and talked and I laughed and talked too. I said to myself that one must always laugh with him. I felt in the right mood for it. 'Laughter and love go together,' as Alain said. It was not a question of love, but of being in harmony with each other. And besides, I was rather proud that Luc thought about me, admired me, and desired me. I could regard myself as rather special, desirable. The little keeper of my conscience, who, whenever I thought about myself, showed me a pitiable reflection, was perhaps too severe, too pessimistic?

When I left Luc I went into a bar and drank another whisky with the four hundred francs put aside for my dinner. After ten minutes I felt wonderfully kind, tender, and attractive. I looked for someone who could benefit by it, so that I could explain to him all the hard, sweet, and painful things I knew about life. I felt as if I could go on talking for hours. The barman was nice, but uninterested, so I went to the café in the Rue Saint-Jacques, where I met Bertrand. He was alone with several saucers in front of him. I sat next to him and he looked very pleased to see me.

'I was just thinking of you. There's a new bebop orchestra at the Kentucky. What if we went there? It's ages since we danced together.'

'I haven't a sou,' I said regretfully.

'My mother gave me ten thousand francs the other day, so we'll have another drink and go there.'

'But it's only eight o'clock,' I said, 'and it doesn't start till ten.'

'We'll go on drinking then,' said Bertrand gaily.

I was delighted. I enjoyed dancing difficult bebop steps with Bertrand. The juke-box was playing a jazz tune that made me move my legs in rhythm with it. When Bertrand had paid for the drinks I began to realize that he had already drunk a lot. He was in high spirits. In any case he was my best friend, my brother, and I loved him.

We did a round of bars until ten o'clock and were quite drunk at the end. Very gay, but not sentimental. When we got to the Kentucky the orchestra was starting to play. There was hardly anyone there and we had the floor to ourselves. Contrary to what I had expected, we danced well, and were very relaxed. I loved that music and the stimulus it gave me and the pleasure of following the rhythm of it with my whole body. We only sat down to drink.

'Music,' I said confidentially to Bertrand, 'jazz music gives one a heightened sense of being free from care.'

He stopped suddenly:

'That's it exactly! Most interesting. Excellent definition, bravo, Dominique!'

'But it is so,' I added.

'Awful whisky at the Kentucky! Good music, however. Music spells freedom from worry.'

'Worry about what? Listen to the trumpet. It's not only free from worry but it is necessary to the band. It was necessary to hold that note to the end. You felt it? Necessary, like love, like physical love. There's a moment when there must be . . . it cannot be otherwise.'

'I quite agree, most interesting. Shall we dance?'

We spent the night dancing, drinking, and exchanging platitudes. Finally there was a vortex of faces, of feet, and there was Bertrand's arm which threw me away from him and the music which threw me back towards him, and the overwhelming heat and the suppleness of our bodies.

'It's four a.m. Closing time,' said Bertrand.

'At my home too,' I remarked.

'It doesn't matter,' he said.

It was true it did not matter. We went back to his rooms and we lay on his bed, and it was quite normal that, just as in the winter, I should feel Bertrand's familiar weight and we would be happy together.

8

He lay beside me still asleep, his hip touching mine. It must have been early in the morning. I could not get to sleep again and I began thinking that I felt as far away from him as he was from me in his dreams. My real self seemed to be beyond the suburban houses, fields, and trees of my childhood, standing motionless at the end of a long avenue. It was as if the young girl leaning over the sleeper were a pale reflection of the calm and relentless figure whose shell I had discarded to live my own life.

I stretched myself and dressed. Bertrand woke up, questioned me, yawned, and passed his hand over his cheeks and chin, grumbling about his beard. I arranged to meet him in the evening, and went back to my room to work. But in vain. It was almost midday and atrociously hot. I was lunching with Luc and Françoise, and it was too late to start work now. I went out once more to buy a packet of cigarettes, came in, smoked one, and suddenly realized that not one of my movements had been conscious the whole morning, that during all those hours I had merely been obeying a vague instinct to carry on as usual. For me there was no reality in the wonderful smile in the omnibus, nor in the palpitating life of the streets, and I did not love Bertrand. I needed somebody or something. Lighting another cigarette, I whispered to myself 'somebody or something', and it sounded rather odd and melodramatic. So now, like Catherine, I had my moments of exaggerated sentimentality. I was in love with the word love, and all the words appertaining to it: tender, cruel, sweet, confiding, excessive, and I loved nobody, except perhaps Luc, when he was there. But since the previous day I had not dared think about him. I did not like the taste of renunciation which filled my throat when I remembered him.

I was waiting for Luc and Françoise when I felt a strange nausea which made me hurry to the basin. After it was over, I raised my head and looked at myself in the glass. I had already counted the days: 'So it has happened!' I said aloud. The well-known nightmare that I had gone through so often mistakenly was beginning again. Could it be the whisky I had drunk the night before, I wondered? In that case there was nothing to worry about. I began a grim argument with myself whilst still peering into the mirror with a mixture of curiosity and contempt. I was probably caught in a trap. I would tell Françoise; somehow she would manage to rescue me!

But I did not dare to tell Françoise. Luc gave us some wine for lunch and I grew less worried and tried to reason with myself. How was I to know whether Bertrand, who was so jealous of Luc, had not planned this in order to keep me? I thought I had all the symptoms.

The next day saw the beginning of an early summer heat-wave worse than I had ever known. I walked about the streets, because my room was unbearably hot. I asked Catherine in a roundabout way about possible solutions to my problem without daring to confess anything to her. I did not want to see Luc any more, or Françoise: they were free and strong. I was like a trapped animal, ill, and constantly breaking into hysterical laughter. I had no plans, and no strength. At the end of a week I was certain I was expecting Bertrand's child, and I began to feel calmer. I would have to do something about it. But the day before the examinations I knew that I had been mistaken and it was only a nightmare. I passed the written examination laughing with relief. I had thought of nothing else for ten days and suddenly everything became wonderful again; once more life was gay and full of possibilities.

By chance Françoise came up to my room, was horrified to find it so hot, and proposed that I should go to them to prepare my oral exam. I worked on the white carpet in their apartment, the shutters half-closed, alone. Françoise came in at about five o'clock, showed me what she had bought, questioned me a little about my work, and then we would start joking. Luc would enter the room a little later and join in our laughter. After dinner they took me home. One day that week Luc returned before Françoise. He came to where I was working and knelt down beside me on the carpet amongst my books. He took me in his arms and without a word kissed me. I rediscovered his mouth as if it had been the only one I had ever known, and as if I had been thinking of nothing else for the past fortnight. Then he told me he would write to me during the holidays, and that if I liked we could meet somewhere for a week. He caressed my neck and searched for my mouth. I longed to stay there lying against his shoulder until it got dark, perhaps complaining a little that we did not love each other. The scholastic year was over.

PART TWO

9

The house was long and grey. A field stretched down from it to the green, sluggish River Yonne, which was guarded by flights of swallows and poplars. One in particular I loved to lie under, with my feet propped up on its trunk, looking upwards at the branches swaying in the wind. The earth smelt of warm grass and this never ceased to give me pleasure, a pleasure combined with a sense of my own helplessness. I knew that countryside in sunshine and in rain, long before I knew Paris with its streets, the Seine, and men; it was unchanging.

By some miracle I had passed my exams and now had time to read. I used to walk slowly back to the house for meals. Fifteen years earlier my mother had lost a son in somewhat tragic circumstances, and her subsequent neurasthenia had gradually become part of the house itself. The sadness that permeated the walls had assumed a pious flavour. My father tiptoed about carrying shawls for my mother.

I had a curious letter from Bertrand, full of allusions to the night we had spent together after going to the Kentucky. He said he was afraid he had been lacking in respect for me. He had not seemed to me to have been any different, and as our intimate relations had always been natural and satisfying, I could not imagine what he meant. At last I realized he was trying to insinuate that there was something of a particularly erotic nature between us which ought to bind us closer together. I thought this rather contemptible, and was annoyed with him for trying to complicate what had been the happiest and perhaps the purest side of our friendship. I understood that he was catching at a straw, so to speak, in order to avoid facing the plain truth, namely, that I did not love him any more.

I had not heard from Luc during that month. There had only been a card from Françoise to which he had added his signature. I kept telling myself, with a sort of stupid pride, that I did not love him, the proof being that I had not suffered from our separation. I did not realize that if this had been true I should have been saddened instead of triumphant. I had no patience for all these fine distinctions. I thought I had myself well under control.

I liked being in my parents' home, though logically I should have been very bored. In a way I was bored, but pleasantly, and not ashamed of it as I was with the people in Paris. I was very nice and polite to everyone, and happy to be so. It was such a relief to have nothing to do but wander from one room to another, and from one field to the next, letting the days drift idly by, and gradually acquiring a pale brown tan over face and body. I read and I waited, without waiting, for the holidays to end. They were like an enormous blank in my life.

At last, after two months, Luc's letter came. He said he would be in Avignon on the 22nd September, and would wait for me, or I could write to him there. I decided at once to go, and the past months appeared in retrospect to have been a paradise of simplicity. It was just like Luc: his quiet and apparently indifferent tone, and the ridiculous, unexpected suggestion of Avignon as a meeting place. I concocted a story for my parents, and wrote to Catherine, asking her to send me a false invitation. When it came, it was with a letter expressing her surprise, as Bertrand was in the south of France with some of our friends, and who else would I be meeting? Catherine was very upset at my lack of confidence in her, and she knew of no reason which would justify it. I wrote her a few words of thanks, telling her that if she wished to hurt Bertrand, she had only to mention my letter, which she did, out of friendship to him, of course.

Carrying a small suitcase, I took the train to Avignon, which was fortunately on the line to the coast. My parents saw me off. Without knowing why, I had tears in my eyes. It seemed to me that for the first time I was leaving my childhood, with its familiar security, behind, and I already hated Avignon.

After Luc's long silence and the cool tone of his letter I had a picture of him as rather hard and indifferent and I arrived at Avignon prepared to be on my guard, not a favourable attitude for a lovers' meeting. I was not going away with Luc because he loved me, nor because I loved him, but because we understood and liked each other. On second thoughts these reasons seemed insufficient, and the whole trip terrifying.

But once again Luc surprised me. He was waiting on the station platform looking very worried, but as soon as he saw me his face lighted up. When I got off the train he put his arms round me and kissed me lightly.

'You look marvellous! I'm so glad you've come.'

'You too,' I said, referring to his appearance. He was thinner, sunburnt, and much better looking than in Paris.

'There's no reason why we should stay in Avignon. Let's go and have a look at the sea; that is what we're here for. Later we'll decide what we want to do.'

His car stood in front of the station. He threw my suitcase into the back and we drove off. I felt completely stunned and, perversely enough, a little disappointed because he was so unlike what I had expected. I hadn't remembered him so seductive nor so gay.

The road was beautiful, bordered with plane trees. Luc smoked, and we raced along in the sunshine with the hood down. I said to myself: 'Well, here I am, it is really happening!'

And it meant nothing to me, absolutely nothing. I might just as well have been sitting under my poplar tree with a book. My lack of comprehension for what was actually taking place soon struck me as funny, and I asked Luc for a cigarette. He smiled.

'Better now?'

I began to laugh.

'Yes, much better. I'm wondering what I am doing here beside you, that's all.'

'You're not doing anything: you're out for a drive, you're smoking, you're wondering if you are not going to be rather bored. Would you like me to kiss you?'

He stopped the car, took me by the shoulders, and kissed me. For us, this was a very good beginning. I smiled a little, and we continued on our way. He was holding my hand. He understood me. For two months I had been living with people who were semi-strangers, who existed in an atmosphere of perpetual mourning which I did not share, and now it seemed that life was slowly beginning again.

The sea was a great surprise to me. For a moment I regretted that Françoise was not there so that I could tell her that it really was blue with red rocks and yellow sands and that it looked marvellous. I was a little afraid Luc might show it to me with an air of triumph, while he watched my reactions, which would have forced me to answer in superlatives, but he just pointed to it with a finger when we reached Saint-Raphaël:

'There's the sea!'

We drove on slowly through the evening, the sea gradually fading to grey. At Cannes, Luc stopped the car on the Croisette in front of a gigantic hotel. The entrance-hall terrified me. I knew that before I could feel at ease I would have to get accustomed to all this grandeur, all the lackeys, and transform them into familiar sights, which would no longer be a menace to me. I wished I were far away. Luc, who was conferring with a haughty-looking man behind a desk, noticed my discomfort, and guided me through the hall with a hand on my shoulder. The room was immense, almost white, with two balcony doors overlooking the sea. There was a confusion of porters, luggage, windows and cupboards being opened. I stood in the middle of it with dangling arms, disgusted at my incapacity to react.

'Here we are,' said Luc.

He gave a satisfied glance at the room and went out on to the balcony.

'Come and have a look.'

I leaned on the balustrade beside him, but kept a respectable distance. I had no desire to look out, nor to be so familiar with this man I hardly knew. He glanced briefly at me: 'Now look here, you little savage, go and have a bath and then come and have a drink with me. In your case I think the only remedies are comfort and alcohol.'

He was right. I came back when I was dressed, with a glass in my hand, complimented him on all his arrangements, on the bathroom and the sea. He told me I was looking very pretty. I answered that he was very good-looking, and we surveyed the crowd and the palms with satisfaction. Then he went in to change, leaving me with a second whisky, and I walked about barefoot on the thick carpet humming to myself.

Dinner was very pleasant. We talked sensibly and affectionately of Françoise and Bertrand. I hoped I wouldn't meet Bertrand, but Luc said we were sure to run into someone who would be delighted to be able to tell him and Françoise that they had seen us, and that we should put off worrying about it until we were back in Paris. I was touched that he took such a risk for my sake. I yawned because I was dead tired, and I added that I admired the way he took everything in his stride.

'It's wonderful! You make up your mind to do a thing, you do it, and accept the consequences, you're not afraid.'

'What should I be afraid of?' he asked with a strange sadness in his voice. 'Bertrand won't kill me, Françoise won't leave me, you won't love me.'

'Perhaps Bertrand will kill me, though,' I said crossly.

'He's much too kind,' said Luc. 'In fact, everyone is kind.'

'It's the bad ones who cause the most trouble, isn't that what you once said?'

'Quite right. But it's late, come to bed.'

He said it quite naturally. Our conversation had been far from passionate, and that 'come to bed' seemed to me rather bold. To tell the truth I was frightened, very frightened of the night before me.

In the bathroom I put on my pyjamas with trembling hands. They were like schoolgirl's, but I had no others. When I entered the room Luc was already in bed. He was facing the window, smoking. I slipped in beside him. He stretched out his hand and took mine. I was shivering.

'Take off your pyjamas, little idiot, you'll get them all crushed. How can you be cold on a night like this? Are you ill?'

He took me in his arms, carefully peeled off my pyjamas, and threw them in a heap on the floor. I remarked that they would get crushed all the same. He laughed gently. All his movements had become very gentle. He gently kissed my shoulders and my mouth, while he continued to talk:

'You smell of warm grass. Do you like this room? Otherwise we'll go somewhere else. Cannes is a nice place . . .'

I answered 'Yes, yes' in a strangled voice. I was longing for it to be tomorrow morning. It was not until he moved a little away from me and placed a hand on my side that I became really concerned. He caressed me and I kissed his neck, his chest, everything I could touch of that black shadow outlined against the window. I put my hands on his back; we sighed. Then I saw nothing more. I was dying, I was about to die, and yet I did not die, but I swooned. The rest of the world faded into insignificance, as it always will.

When we separated, Luc opened his eyes and smiled at me. I fell asleep immediately, with my head on his arm.

I had always heard that it is very difficult to live with anyone and I believed it in theory, though I did not actually experience it during the short time I spent with Luc. I thought it must be true, because I never felt at my ease with him: I was afraid of his being bored. Usually I am more frightened of being bored myself than of boring others, but in this case the situation was reversed, and I found it rather a strain. How could Luc be difficult to live with, considering that he said very little and did not even ask me what I was thinking about, as most people do? He invariably looked pleased to have me with him, made no demands on me, and showed no signs either of indifference or passion. We walked in step, had the same tastes, the same rhythm of life; we liked being together, and all went well between us. I did not even regret too much that he could not make the tremendous effort needed to love someone, to know them, and to dispel their loneliness. We were friends and lovers. We bathed in the too-blue Mediterranean together, lunched almost in silence, stupefied by the sun, and then returned to the hotel. Sometimes as I lay in his arms in that moment of great tenderness that follows love-making I longed to say: 'Luc, love me, let's try, do try!' but I never did. I confined myself to kissing his eyes, his mouth, all the features in that new face which the lips discover after the eyes have feasted on it. I had never loved a face so much. I even loved his cheeks: that part of the face which, until then, had always seemed lifeless to me, fish-like. When I laid my face against Luc's cool cheek, a little roughened by the growing bristles, I understood why Proust had written at such length of Albertine's cheeks. He also taught me to know my body, and talked quite dispassionately about it, as of something precious. Sensuality was not the basis of our relationship, but something else, a strange bond that united us against the weariness of playing a part, the weariness of talking, in short: weariness itself.

After dinner we always strolled round to the same rather sinister little bar behind the Rue d'Antibes. There was a small band, and when we first went there Luc asked them to play 'Lone and Sweet' for me, as he knew I liked it. Afterwards he turned to me with an air of triumph:

'Is that the tune you wanted?'

'Yes, it's nice of you to have thought of it.'

'Does it remind you of Bertrand?'

I answered that it did, a little, but that the record had been in every juke-box for ages. He looked rather cross.

'What a pity, we'll have to find another.'

'Why?'

'When one has a love affair there must be a special tune, a perfume, something to remind one of it for the future.'

My expression must have amused him, for he began to laugh:

'At your age one never thinks of the future. I'm looking forward to a pleasant old age, with my records.'

'Have you many?'

'No.'

'What a pity!' I exclaimed. 'If I were your age I should prob-ably have a whole library of them.'

He took my hand.

'Are you offended?'

'No, but all the same, it seems strange to think that in a few years' time, a whole week of my life, that I lived with a man, will have been reduced to a gramophone record; especially when that man is quite certain of it and says so.'

I was so irritated that tears came into my eyes. It was the way he had said 'Are you offended?' When people used a certain tone towards me it always made me feel like crying.

'Otherwise I'm not offended,' I said in a shaky voice.

'Let's dance,' said Luc.

He took my arm and we began to dance to Bertrand's tune, which was not nearly so well played as on the records.

While we were dancing. Luc suddenly held me very close, I suppose to show his violent affection. I, too, clung to him. Then he let me go and we spoke of other things. We soon found a tune that suited us, which was quite easy because it was being played everywhere. Except for that slight argument I behaved very well; I was gay, and thought our little adventure was proving a great success. Besides, I admired Luc. I could not help admiring his intelligence, his equilibrium, his virile way of giving to each thing its right weight and importance, without being either cynical or complacent. Sometimes in exasperation I wanted to say to him: 'Why can't you love me? It would be so much more restful for me.' But I knew this was impossible. Ours was more an affinity than a passion, and neither of us could ever bear to be dominated by the other. Luc had neither the opportunity, the strength, nor the desire for a closer relationship.

The week we had planned was nearly over, but Luc said nothing about leaving. We had become very brown, but were tired after nights spent in the bar, talking, drinking, and waiting for the dawn: the pale dawn over an inhuman sea, the motionless boats, the mad, graceful crowd of gulls roosting on the hotel roof. We went back at dawn, greeted the same sleepy porter, and Luc took me in his arms and loved me in a state of semi-intoxication and fatigue. We woke at midday for our bathe.

That morning, which would have been our last, I imagined he was in love with me. He walked about the room with a thoughtful expression that intrigued me.

'What did you tell your family? When did you say you were coming back?'

'I told them in about a week.'

'If you like, we could stay on another week.'

'Yes,' I said. 'Do let's.'

I realized I had not seriously thought about leaving. I would pass my life in that hotel which had become so hospitable, so comfortable, like a great ship. All my nights with Luc would be sleepless, we would drift slowly from summer to winter, and towards death, always talking of the temporary nature of our stay.

'But I thought Françoise was expecting you?'

'I can arrange that,' he said. 'I don't want to leave Cannes, or you.'

'Neither do I,' I said quietly.

For a moment I imagined that perhaps he loved me, but did not want to tell me so. It made my heart miss a beat. Then I thought, what did words matter, he cared for me, and that was enough. We were going to have one more happy week together. Afterwards I would have to leave him. But why, for whom, for what? To go back to my usual boredom and loneliness? Now, when he looked at me, it was his face I saw; when he spoke, it was he I tried to understand. He it was who interested me, whose happiness I had at heart: Luc, my lover.

'It's a good idea,' I said. 'To tell you the truth, I hadn't thought about leaving.'

'You never think of anything,' he said with a laugh.

'Not when I'm with you,' I said.

'Why? Do you feel so young and irresponsible?'

He smiled mockingly. If I had shown him that I wanted it

otherwise he would soon have changed his 'little girl and her protector' attitude. Fortunately I felt quite adult, even rather blasé.

'No,' I said, 'I feel perfectly responsible. But what am I supposed to be responsible for? There is only myself, and my own life, which, after all, is simple enough. Still, I am not unhappy, I'm sometimes even contented, but never really happy. I am nothing, except when I'm with you, and then I'm all right!'

'That's good!' he said, 'I feel the same with you.'

'Let's start purring!'

He began to laugh:

'You're like a cat with its back up as soon as you think you might be deprived of your absurd little dose of daily despair. I should hate to make you "purr", as you say. I don't want you to be "in heaven" when you are with me, it would bore me to extinction.'

'Why?'

'I'd feel lonely. That is the only time I'm ever frightened by Françoise: when she's next to me, saying nothing, and feeling satisfied. On the other hand, it is very satisfying to a man to feel he has made a woman happy, even if he can't imagine why.'

'Well, what could be better?' I said quickly. 'When we get back, you'll make Françoise happy, and me a little unhappy.'

I regretted my words as soon as I had spoken. He turned to me:

'You, unhappy?'

'No,' I said, smiling, 'only somewhat bewildered. I shall have to find somebody to look after me, and no one could do it as well as you.'

'I'd rather not know about it,' he said angrily. Then he thought again; 'Yes, you had better tell me. You must always tell me everything. If the fellow is troublesome, I'll thrash him, otherwise I'll sing his praises, like a real father.'

He took my hand, turned it over, and kissed the palm very gently. I put my free arm round his neck. I thought how young he still was, how vulnerable, and how kind: this man with whom I was having an unsentimental love affair with no future. And he was honest.

'We're both honest people,' I said sententiously.

'Yes,' he said, laughing, 'but don't smoke your cigarette like that if you want to look like an honest woman!'

I drew myself up in my spotted dressing-gown:

'Well, if I'm an honest woman, what am I doing here, dressed in this way in a palace hotel with another woman's husband? Am I not a typical example of one of those vicious young ladies from Saint-Germain-des-Prés who break up marriages as a hobby?'

'Yes, and I'm the model husband, who has been led astray by my senses. I am the victim, the unhappy victim! Come to bed.'

'No,' I said, 'I refuse. I have lighted the flame, but I will not be the one to extinguish it, so there!'

He collapsed on to the bed with his head in his hands. I sat next to him, looking grave, and when he raised his head I fixed my eyes on him severely.

'I'm a vamp!'

'And what am I?'

'A miserable human wreck, who was once a man . . . Luc, we have another week!'

I threw myself down beside him. I entwined my hair with his. His skin was warm and fresh against mine, he smelt of the sea and salt.

I was lying on a deck-chair near some elderly English ladies facing the sea in front of the hotel. It was eleven o'clock in the morning. Luc had to go to Nice on business, and although I liked Nice, at least the old part, between the station and the

Promenade des Anglais, I had refused to go with him because I suddenly longed to be by myself.

So there I was, yawning (for I was exhausted from lack of sleep) and extremely comfortable. My hand trembled a little as I struck a match to light my cigarette. The September sun, no longer very hot, caressed my cheek. For once I was delighted to be alone. 'We're only happy when we're tired,' Luc once said, and it was true that I was one of those people who are only happy once they have subdued that part of their vitality which continually makes demands and always feels misgivings: the part which asks 'What have you done with your life? What are you going to make of it?' Questions to which I could only reply 'Nothing.'

A very beautiful young man passed by at that moment. My glance travelled over him with a new and wonderful indifference. Usually I was rather embarrassed by beauty that seemed to me too blatant and inaccessible. The young man, though his appearance was so pleasing, did not exist for me. Luc was the only man who was real for me, but I was not the only woman for him. He looked at them complacently, but without comment.

Suddenly I could only see the sea through a mist. I was suffocating. I felt my forehead, it was soaked with perspiration and the roots of my hair were damp. A drop ran slowly down my spine. Perhaps death was like this: a blue mist into which one gradually sinks. I would not have offered any resistance to death at that moment.

The thought had come into my mind for a fleeting second. I seized upon it: 'I would not mind dying.' All the same, there were things I cared for: Paris, the scent of flowers, books, love, and the life I was living with Luc. I had the feeling I would never again be so happy as with him. He had been meant for me since the beginning of time, and if there were such a thing as destiny, then we had been fated to meet. My destiny was that

Luc would leave me, and I would have to try to start all over again with someone else, but I would never again feel as I did with him: so tranquil, so little alone, and so free to say what I thought, knowing he would understand. But he was going back to his wife, leaving me to my room in Paris, to those interminable afternoons, my moments of despair, and to my unsatisfactory love affairs. I began to weep out of self-pity.

After a few minutes I blew my nose. Sitting quite near me I noticed an elderly Englishwoman staring fixedly at me. I felt myself blushing. Then I looked more carefully at her. I was filled with respect: here was another human being, she was looking at me and I at her, both staring hard at each other in the sunshine, both almost on the threshold of some great revelation, two human beings, not even speaking the same language, two perfect strangers. Soon she got up and, leaning heavily on a stick, limped away.

Happiness is like a flat plain without landmarks. That is why I have no precise memories of my stay in Cannes except those few unhappy moments, Luc's laughter, and the pathetic scent of fading mimosa in our room at night. Perhaps, for people like myself, happiness signifies a bolder attitude towards the tedium of everyday existence. Just then I realized so well what it meant to me. For when I met Luc's glance I felt that all was well with my world, he was taking my worries off my shoulders. When he smiled at me, I knew why he was smiling, and felt like smiling too.

I remember an exciting moment one morning. Luc was lying on the sand, while I was diving from a raft. I climbed up to the highest board. I could see Luc and the crowds on the beach, and below me the calm water, into which I was about to fall as though it were silk. I would be falling from a great height, and during my descent I would be alone, terribly alone. Luc was watching me. He made an ironical gesture to pretend he was frightened, and I let myself go. The sea rose up to meet me and I hurt myself as I dived in. I swam ashore and collapsed on the sand next to Luc, sprinkling him with water. I laid my head on his dry back and kissed his shoulder.

'Are you crazy, or just trying to set up a record?' he asked.

'Crazy,' I answered.

'That was my proud thought when I saw you diving from so high in order to come back to me. It made me very happy.'

'Are you happy? I am. I must be because I never have to ask myself the question. That's an axiom, isn't it?' All I could see of him was his firm brown neck because he was lying face downwards. 'Anyway, I'm returning you to Françoise in good condition.'

'Cynic!' he answered.

'You are far less cynical than we are,' I replied. 'Women are very cynical. You're just a little boy compared with Françoise and me.'

'Don't be so pretentious.'

'You men are more pretentious than we are,' I said. 'Pretentious women are merely ridiculous; in men it takes the form of a sham virility which they exploit in order to . . .'

'Have you finished with all your axioms? Talk to me about the weather, it's the only subject permitted on holidays.'

'It is very, very fine,' I said, and turning on to my back, I went to sleep.

When I woke up, the sky was overcast, the beach deserted, and I was utterly exhausted. Luc was sitting beside me fully dressed, smoking and looking at the sea. I watched him for a moment without revealing that I was awake. For the first time I felt a purely objective curiosity about him: 'what can he be thinking of?' I wondered, 'what does a human being think about on an empty beach, facing an empty sea, beside someone fast asleep?' I put out my hand and touched his arm. He did not even start. He was never startled, rarely surprised, and seldom raised his voice.

'So you've woken up?' he said lazily. He stretched himself. 'It's four o'clock.' I sat up.

'Four o'clock? Do you mean to say I've been asleep for four hours?'

'Don't get excited,' said Luc. 'We have nothing particular to do.'

His words struck me as ominous. It was true we had nothing to do when we were together, no work, no friends in common. 'Do you regret it?' I asked him.

He turned to me and smiled. 'I love it! Put on your sweater, darling, you'll catch cold. Let's have tea at the hotel.'

The Croisette was gloomy now the sun had gone in; a slight breeze stirred the ancient palms, the hotel seemed to be asleep. We had tea brought up. I had a hot bath and then lay down beside Luc, who was reading on the bed, from time to time flicking the ash from his cigarette. We had closed the shutters to exclude the grey sky outside: the room was warm and cosy. I lay on my back with my hands crossed on my stomach like a corpse or a fat man. I shut my eyes. The only sounds were the rustle of pages as Luc turned them and the distant splash of waves.

I was thinking: 'I am close to Luc, lying beside him. I have only to put out my hand to touch him. I am familiar with his body, his voice, the way he sleeps. Now he's reading and I'm just a little bored, but it's not disagreeable. Soon we'll be having dinner, then we shall go to bed, and in three days we must part. It will probably never again be like this. But this moment is ours. I don't know if it is love, or whether we just harmonize, and it is not important. We are alone, but separate. He has no idea I am thinking of us; he's reading. But we're together, and I have all he can give me either of his warmth or indifference. In six months, when we shall perhaps no longer meet, I shall have forgotten this moment and only remember others, involuntary, vague and silly ones perhaps, and yet this is the moment I shall probably have loved most, the one when I accepted that life was just what it seemed, both peaceful and heart-rending.' I stretched out my arm and took the book away from Luc. It was *La Famille Fenouillard*, and he was always telling me I ought to read it. I began to laugh, and he joined in while we read together, cheek to cheek, and soon mouth to mouth, the book at last falling to the floor, pleasure enveloping us like the night over Cannes.

At last came the day of departure. We had avoided all mention of it during the last evening because we were both afraid, he that I would become sentimental, and I, that, feeling he was half-expecting it, I would give way. During the night I woke up several times in a panic and felt for him, to make sure he was still there, sleeping beside me. And on each occasion, as if he had been on the watch, or as if he were sleeping so lightly that he was conscious of my fears, he took me in his arms, put a hand on my neck, and murmured: 'There, there,' as one does to reassure an animal. It was a warm night of half-sleep, broken by whispers, heavy with the scent of the mimosa we were leaving behind us. Then came the morning and breakfast, and Luc packed his bag. I did mine at the same time, and we discussed the route we would take and the restaurants on the way. I was annoyed with myself for pretending to be calm and brave when I was not brave, and saw no reason why I should be. I felt nothing except perhaps a vague unease. For once we were each playing a part. I thought it wiser to stick to it, for I did not want to start suffering before I left him; far better to adopt the attitude, the movements, and the face of decent mediocrity.

'Well, are we ready?' he said at last. 'I'll ring for them to fetch the luggage.'

I became fully conscious of the moment.

'Let's go out on to the balcony for the last time,' I said in a melodramatic voice.

He looked upset, then, seeing my expression, began to laugh.

'You're a tough nut, a cynic. I like you.'

We were standing in the middle of the room. He put his arms round me and shook me gently: 'You know it is a rare thing to be able to say to someone: "I like you," after two weeks' cohabitation.'

'It wasn't cohabitation,' I protested laughing; 'it was a honeymoon.'

'All the more reason,' he said, moving away from me.

At that moment I felt he was leaving me, and I longed to hold him back by the lapels of his coat. It was a fleeting thought, and it shook me.

On the return journey I drove part of the way. Luc said we would arrive in Paris during the night, that he would ring me up the next day, and he would arrange a lunch with Françoise, now home after two weeks in the country with her mother. I didn't like the idea of meeting Françoise so soon, but Luc told me to say nothing about our trip and that he would arrange everything with her. I could see myself spending the autumn with them both, and meeting Luc sometimes for a stolen kiss or a night. I had never counted on his leaving Françoise, first because he had warned me, and then because I realized it was out of the question to hurt her. Even if he had offered to do so, I would probably not have accepted it at that moment.

He told me he had a lot of work waiting to be dealt with, but that he was not very interested in it. As for me, the new term was beginning, and I would have to go on with the studies that had so depressed me before. We were both in low spirits when we reached Paris, but I did not mind because it was the same for both of us: the same discouragement, the same weariness, and consequently the same necessity to hold on to each other.

We arrived in Paris late in the night. At the Porte d'Italie I glanced at Luc, who looked tired, and I thought that we had managed our little escapade very well. After all, we were adult, civilized, and reasonable. I suddenly felt furiously, horribly humiliated.

PART THREE

II

Paris was never strange to me when I returned to it, I always felt at home there. Once again I was captivated by its charm as I walked about the streets, still deserted after the summer. Paris distracted me during the three long empty days of Luc's absence. I was always searching for him, and seeking his hand at night, and each time not finding him seemed unnatural and unnecessary. In retrospect the two weeks with him appeared to me both satisfying and bitter. Strangely enough, I had no sense of defeat, but rather one of achievement, and this, I realized, would make it difficult, and perhaps painful for me to hope for any similar experience.

Bertrand would soon be home. What should I say to him? I knew he would try to get me back. Should I renew our intimacy? And, above all, how could I bear the close contact of anyone but Luc?

Luc did not telephone the following day, nor the day after. I attributed this to complications with Françoise and felt rather important, but also ashamed. I walked a great deal, and thought in a vague way about the coming year. Perhaps I could find something more interesting to work at than law? Luc had said he wanted to introduce me to one of his friends, the editor of a newspaper. Until then, with my usual inertia, I had resorted to sentimentality as a compensation for my troubles; now I looked to a profession instead.

After two days I could no longer resist the desire to see Luc. Not daring to telephone, I sent a little note, asking him to ring me up. He did so the following day, and said he had fetched Françoise from the country and could not telephone to me before. His voice sounded rather strained. I thought it was because he missed me. When, a moment afterwards, he told me so, I had a vision of a café where we would meet, and he would take me in his arms, saying he couldn't live without me, that the past two days had been unbearable. I would have replied truthfully that I felt the same and left the decision to him. But when we actually met in a café, he told me that Françoise was well, that she had asked no questions, and that he was overwhelmed with work. He said: 'You look lovely!' and kissed the palm of my hand.

I found him changed by his dark suit, and attractive. His face looked sharpened and tired. It seemed strange that he was no longer mine. I was already beginning to think that I had not really 'benefited' (I disliked the word) by my stay with him. I talked quite cheerfully, and so did he, but we were both unnatural: perhaps because we were surprised that one can so easily live together for two weeks without anything serious happening. When he got up I felt suddenly indignant, and almost said to him: 'Where are you going? Are you leaving me alone?' He left, and I was alone. I had nothing much to do. I thought: 'How silly all this is!' and shrugged my shoulders. I walked about the streets for an hour, went into one or two cafés, hoping to meet some friends, but no one had come back yet. I could still go and spend a fortnight on the Yonne, but as I was to dine with Luc and Françoise two days later, I decided only to go away after that.

I spent those two days at the cinema or on my bed, sleeping and reading. My room seemed unfamiliar to me. The night of the dinner I dressed carefully and went to their house. As I rang the bell I had a moment of fear, but Françoise came to open the door herself and her smile reassured me at once. I knew, just as

Luc had told me, that she would never be ridiculous, and never play a rôle that was not in keeping with her great kindness and dignity. She had never been betrayed, and never would be.

It was a curious meal. There we were, the three of us, and everything was as before, only we had drunk a good deal. Françoise appeared to know nothing, but I thought she looked at me more attentively than usual. From time to time, Luc spoke to me, looking into my eyes, and I made a point of answering gaily and naturally. The conversation turned upon Bertrand, who was expected back the following week. 'I shan't be here,' I said.

'Where will you be?' said Luc.

'I'm probably going to stay a few days with my parents.'

'When will you be back?' (It was Françoise who asked me.)

'In a fortnight.'

'Dominique, I simply must call you "tu",' she said. 'It's ridiculous to go on saying "vous" to you.'

'Let's all call each other "tu",' said Luc, with a laugh, and he went over to the gramophone. My eyes followed him, and as I turned back to Françoise I saw that she was watching me. I stared back, feeling rather uneasy, but determined not to appear to be avoiding her glance. She put her hand over mine for a moment with a sad little smile which upset me:

'You'll send us a postcard, won't you, Dominique? You haven't told us yet how your mother is?'

'Very well,' I said. 'She . . .'

I stopped because Luc had put on the tune that was played everywhere in Cannes, and suddenly it all came back to me with a shock. He had not turned round. For a moment I felt in a panic between Françoise's complacence, which was not genuine, and Luc's unreal sentimentality. It was all such a muddle. I longed to run away.

'I like that tune,' said Luc quietly.

He sat down, and I realized that he had been thinking of

nothing, not even of our bitter little dispute about keeping records as souvenirs. It was just that the tune must have been going round in his head, and he had bought the record to get it out of his system.

'I like it very much too,' I said.

He raised his eyes to me, remembered, and smiled so tenderly and openly that I lowered mine. Françoise lit a cigarette. I was quite bewildered. Our situation could not even be regarded as false, for surely we need only have mentioned it, for each one to have offered advice, calmly and objectively, as if the matter did not concern ourselves.

'Well, are we going to that play or not?' asked Luc, and he turned to explain to me, 'We've been invited to see a new play. We could all go.'

'Oh, yes,' I said. 'Why not?' I nearly added, with a burst of hysterical laughter: 'the more the merrier.'

Françoise took me to her room to try on one of her coats, more elegant than mine. She put on one or two, and turned me about to see the effect with the collar up. At one moment she was holding it against my face with both hands, and in my hysterical state I thought: 'I'm at her mercy; perhaps she's going to strangle me or bite me.' But she only smiled:

'You're rather lost in it.'

'Quite true,' I answered, not thinking of the coat.

'I simply must see you when you come back.'

That's it, I thought. She's going to ask me not to see Luc any more. Could I agree? I knew that the answer was I could never give him up.

'I've decided to look after you,' Françoise went on, 'to help you to dress better, and to show you something more amusing than all those students and college libraries.'

Oh, good heavens! I thought. This is really not the right moment to say such a thing.

'Wouldn't you like it?' she said, when I did not reply. 'I always feel you might be my daughter' – she said it half-laughing, but kindly – 'even if you are a bundle of nerves and only interested in the intellectual side of life . . .'

'It's too sweet of you,' I said, emphasizing the 'too'. 'I don't know what to do.'

'Leave it all to me,' she said, smiling.

I've got myself into a nice mess, I thought, but if Françoise likes me, and wants to see me, I'll be able to be with Luc oftener. Perhaps I could tell her about him. Perhaps she wouldn't mind much after ten years of marriage.

'What makes you like me so much?' I asked.

'You have the same kind of nature as Luc. You both have a tendency to be unhappy, and need the consolation of a Venus like me. There's no escape for you!'

In imagination I gave up the struggle. Luc was in a very good mood at the theatre. Françoise pointed everyone out to me, and told me all the scandal about each. They took me back to my pension, and Luc openly kissed the palm of my hand, leaving me rather flustered. I soon fell asleep, and the next day I took the train to the Yonne.

12

But the Yonne was grey, and I was intolerably bored. It was not only boredom now, but a longing for someone. At the end of a week I went back to Paris. As I was leaving, my mother suddenly woke up and asked me if I were happy. I assured her that I was, that I liked studying law, was working hard, and had many friends. Reassured, she left me, and returned once more to her melancholy. Not for a moment had I felt the least desire to confide in her as I had the year before. Besides, what could I have told her? I was definitely growing up.

At the pension I found a note from Bertrand asking me to telephone as soon as I returned. No doubt he wanted an explanation from me (I had not much faith in Catherine's discretion) and I owed him that at least. I rang him up and we arranged to meet. In the meantime I went to register at the university restaurant.

At six o'clock I met Bertrand at the café in the Rue Saint-Jacques, and it seemed as though nothing had happened, and everything would begin again. But as soon as he got up and deferentially kissed my cheek I was recalled to reality. I tried in a feeble way to appear light-hearted and frivolous.

'You've grown better-looking,' I said with real sincerity, and with the cynical little thought: what a pity!

'You too,' he said shortly. 'I wanted you to know: Catherine told me everything.'

'What about?'

'Your stay on the Riviera. I imagine you were with Luc, weren't you?'

'Yes,' I said. I was surprised to notice that he did not appear angry, but calm, and rather sad.

'Well, there you are. I'm not a person to be satisfied with a half-share. I still love you: enough to be able to forgive you, but not enough to allow myself the luxury of being jealous, and of being made to suffer again as I did this spring. You must choose between us.'

He had said it all in one breath.

There was no question of a choice. I was in a quandary. According to Luc I had never considered Bertrand as a problem.

'Either you give up seeing Luc, and we go on as we were, or you see him, and we'll just remain good friends, that's all.'

'I see.' I could not think of anything to say. He seemed to have become more mature and serious. I almost admired him. But he meant nothing to me, absolutely nothing. I laid my hand on his:

'I'm really very sorry,' I said, 'I cannot give him up.'

He remained silent for a moment, looking out of the window.

'It's hard for me,' he said.

'I hate to hurt you,' I went on. I was really distressed.

'That's not the worst part,' he said, as if talking to himself. 'When one has made a decision it's all right. It's when one still hangs on . . .' He turned to me. 'Do you love him?'

'Of course not,' I said, irritated. 'There's no question of that. We get on very well, that's all.'

'If you are ever in trouble, I'm here,' he said. 'And I think you will be. You'll see. There's nothing to Luc. He's just a depressive intellectual, no more.'

I thought of Luc's tenderness and his laughter with a surge of joy.

'Believe me.' He added with a sort of excitement: 'In any case I'll always be available, you know, Dominique. I've been very happy with you.'

We were both on the point of tears. He, because everything was over and he must still have had some hope, and I because I felt I was losing my natural protector in order to embark on an unknown adventure. I got up and kissed him lightly:

'Goodbye, Bertrand. Forgive me.'

'Yes, please go!' he said gently.

I left feeling completely demoralized. What a prospect for the New Year!

Catherine was waiting in my room sitting on the bed with a tragic air. She got up when she saw me and held out her hand. I took it without enthusiasm, and sat down.

'I came to apologize, Dominique. Perhaps I ought not to have said anything to Bertrand? What do you think?'

I admired her for asking the question.

'It doesn't matter. It might have been better for me to have told him myself, but it's of no importance.'

'Good.' She sighed with relief.

She sat down again on the bed, looking pleased and excited.

'And now tell me everything!'

I did not reply, but burst out laughing.

'Well really, Catherine, you are the limit! First you dispose of Bertrand, and once he's out of the way, you can't wait to hear something more exciting.'

'Don't make fun of me,' she said, in a 'little girl' voice. 'Tell me all about it.'

'There's nothing to tell,' I replied shortly. 'I spent a fortnight on the Riviera with someone I liked. For various reasons the story ends there.'

'Is he married?' she asked slyly.

'No, a deaf-mute. Well, I must really unpack my suitcase.'

'I'll wait, you'll tell me in time,' she said.

The worst is that perhaps it's true, I thought as I opened my wardrobe, one day when I'm feeling depressed . . .

'Now about me,' Catherine went on, as if she were going to make a revelation, 'I'm in love.'

'With whom? Oh, the last one you told me about, I suppose.'

'If it doesn't interest you . . .'

But she continued her story all the same. I began to arrange my cupboard in a fury. Why did I have such idiotic friends? Luc wouldn't have put up with her for a moment. But what had Luc to do with it? This was my life after all.

'Well, I love him,' she ended.

'What do you mean by love?' I asked with curiosity.

'I don't know; loving, thinking about someone, going out with them. Isn't that it?'

'I can't say. Perhaps.'

I had finished putting everything away, and sat down on the bed, discouraged. Catherine made an effort to be nice.

'Dominique, you're crazy! You never think of anything yourself. Come out with us this evening. I'm going with Jean-Louis, of course, and one of his friends, a very intelligent boy who goes in for literature. It will do you good.'

Anyhow, I did not want to telephone to Luc until the next day. I was tired; my life seemed to be enveloped in a gloomy storm cloud, with Luc at times in the centre as its only stable element. He alone understood and helped me. I needed him.

Yes, I needed him. I could not ask him for anything but, all the same, he was responsible for me in a way. But I must not let him know it. Conventions must be respected, particularly when defying them will injure others.

'Very well,' I said, 'let's go and meet your Jean-Bernard and his clever friend. I'm sick of intelligent people – no, that's not true, but I only care for depressive intellectuals, the other kind get on my nerves.'

'The name is Jean-Louis, not Jean-Bernard,' she corrected me. 'And what do you mean by the other kind?'

'The ones who can't appreciate that,' I said, pointing melodramatically to the window, and to the bitter-sweet sadness of the lowering grey and pink sky.

'All that's no good for you,' said Catherine uneasily; and she held my arm to guide me as we went down the stairs. She was a good friend after all. I couldn't help liking her.

Her Jean-Louis was a good-looking, if rather shady type, but not unpleasing. His friend Alain was far more witty and amusing, with a sharpness to his intelligence, a certain insincerity, and an ability to see other points of view, all of which were lacking in Bertrand. We soon left Catherine and her admirer, whose open display of passion was rather out of place in a café. Alain took me back to my pension, talking of Stendhal and literature in general. My interest was roused for the first time for two years. He was neither handsome nor ugly, quite nondescript. I was glad to accept his invitation for lunch two days ahead, while hoping it would not coincide with Luc's free day. Now my life was centred round Luc, depended on him, and I had no choice but to accept it.

13

I loved Luc, and this was brought home to me very forcibly the first time we spent a night together again. It was in a hotel facing a quayside. He was lying on his back after love-making, and talking with his eyes closed. He said: 'Kiss me,' and I raised myself on one elbow to kiss him. As I bent over him, I felt an absolute conviction that this man was the only thing that mattered in my life, and the knowledge made me quite dizzy. I realized that the almost unbearable pleasure of waiting to kiss him was the true meaning of love. I knew I loved him, and I lay down with my head on his shoulder without kissing him, with a little shiver of fear.

'You're sleepy,' he said, putting a hand on my back, and he laughed, 'you're like a little animal, after love you either go to sleep or feel thirsty.'

'I was thinking that I love you very much.'

'I too,' he said, and he pressed my shoulder. 'When we haven't met for three days why do you call me "vous"?'

'Because I respect you,' I said. 'I respect you and I love you.'

We laughed together.

'No, but seriously,' I continued, as if I had just had a brilliant idea, 'what would you do if I really loved you?'

'But you do really love me,' he said, closing his eyes once more.

'I mean, supposing I could not live without you, if I wanted you to myself all the time . . . ?'

'I would be very worried,' he said, 'not even flattered.'

'And what would you say to me?'

'I would say: "Dominique, ah well . . . Dominique, forgive me."'

I sighed. In any case his reaction was not the usual unpleasant one of the cautious, prudent kind of man, who says 'I warned you'.

'I forgive you in advance,' I said.

'Hand me a cigarette,' he said lazily. 'They are next to you.'

We smoked in silence. I said to myself: there it is. I love him. Probably this love is only an idea of mine and nothing else; but all the same, I see no way out of it.

Nothing else had existed for me during that whole week since Luc had asked me on the telephone: 'Will you be free the night of the fifteenth?' Every few hours I had thought of his words, remembering the casual tone of his voice, and each time I had felt a leap of joy which seemed to rise up and suffocate me. And now I was with him, and time was passing, slowly and inevitably.

'I'm afraid I shall have to go,' he said; 'it's a quarter to five already.'

'Yes,' I said. 'Is Françoise at home?'

'I told her I was going out with some Belgians to Montmartre. But the cabarets must be closing now.'

'What will she say? Five o'clock is rather late, even for Belgians.'

His eyes were still shut: 'I shall go in and say: "Oh those Belgians!" and stretch myself. She'll turn round and say: "The Alka-Seltzer is in the bathroom," and go to sleep again. That's all.'

'I see, and tomorrow you'll make up a story about cabarets and Belgian morals, and so on?'

'Oh, it will just be a repetition. I can't be bothered with lies, or at least I have no time for them.'

'What have you time for?'

'Nothing at all. Neither time, nor strength, nor inclination. If I had been capable of anything at all, I would have loved you.'

'What difference would it have made?'

'None to us. At least I don't think so. Only I should have been unhappy on account of you, whereas now I'm happy.'

I wondered if this referred to what I had said earlier, but he put his hand on my head almost solemnly:

'I can say anything to you. I love that. I could never tell Françoise that I don't really love her, that there is no real and wonderful foundation to our relationship. At the root of it all is my weariness and my boredom. These are firm and solid bases in their way and one can build a lasting union on them. At least they remain unchanged.'

I lifted my head from his shoulder: 'They are . . .' I was about to add: 'nonsense,' because I wanted to protest, but I said nothing.

'What are they? Are you being childish?' he laughed tenderly. 'My poor darling, you are so young and defenceless, and fortunately so disarming, that I am reassured.'

He took me back to the pension. I was to lunch with him, Françoise, and a friend of theirs the next day. I kissed him goodbye through the car window. He looked old and tired, which touched me and for a moment made me love him more.

14

I awoke the next morning full of energy. Lack of sleep always agreed with me. I got out of bed, went to the window, inhaled the Paris air, and lit a cigarette, although I did not want one. Then I lay down again after glancing at myself in the mirror. I thought I looked rather interesting with my tired eyes. I decided to ask my landlady to heat the room the next day: 'It's icy cold in here!' I said aloud, and my voice sounded strange and husky. 'My dear Dominique,' I went on, 'you have a mania, you really must treat it: plenty of walks, careful reading, young people, perhaps a little light work . . .' I couldn't help being sorry for myself, but luckily I had a sense of humour. I was strong and healthy, why shouldn't I be in love? Besides, I was lunching with the object of my affections. So I went to Luc and Françoise, fortified by a physical well-being, the cause of which I knew.

I caught the bus with a flying leap, and the conductor, with the pretext of helping me up, took advantage of it to put an arm round my waist. I gave him my ticket and we exchanged an understanding smile such as may pass between a man and a woman on these occasions. I stayed on the platform holding the rail, while the bus went bumping along the street. I felt wonderful: I liked the sensation of tautness between my jaw and my solar plexus that I have after a sleepless night.

An unknown friend had already come when I arrived at Françoise's. He was a fat, red-faced man with a dry manner.

Luc was not there. Françoise told us he had spent the night in Montmartre with some Belgian clients, and had only got up at ten o'clock. Those Belgians were really a nuisance, they always wanted to go to Montmartre! I saw the fat man looking at me, and felt myself blush.

Luc came in looking tired.

'Hallo, Pierre, how are you?' he said.

'Weren't you expecting me?'

His manner was somewhat aggressive. Perhaps because Luc showed no surprise at my presence, but only at his.

'Of course I was, my dear fellow,' said Luc, with an exasperated little smile. 'Isn't there anything to drink here? What is that lovely yellow stuff in your glass, Dominique?'

'A neat whisky,' I answered; 'don't you recognize it any more?'

'No,' he said, sitting down on the edge of a chair, as one does in a station. Then he gave us all a glance, still like a traveller, absent-minded and indifferent. He had the air of a spoilt child. Françoise began to laugh:

'My poor Luc, you look almost as ill as Dominique. As for you, my dear girl, I'm going to put a stop to all this. I shall tell Bertrand to . . .'

She told us what she would say to Bertrand. I had not looked at Luc. Thank heaven there was never any conspiracy between us regarding Françoise. It even had its funny side: we spoke of her between ourselves as of a very dear child who caused us a certain amount of worry.

'That sort of fun is no good for anyone,' said Pierre. I suddenly realized that he knew about us, which explained his earlier look of contempt, his dry manner, and those half-allusions. Then I remembered that we had seen him in Cannes, and Luc had mentioned his being in love with Françoise. Now he was outraged, and was sure to tell Françoise. Like Catherine, he would want to hide nothing from his friends, do them a good turn, not abuse their hospitality. And if Françoise should find out and look at me with anger and contempt, and all those other feelings so unsuited to her, and, it seemed, so undeserved by me, then what would I do?

'Let's have lunch,' said Françoise; 'I'm starving.'

We walked to a nearby restaurant. Françoise took my arm, and the men followed.

'How mild it is,' she said, 'I adore the autumn.'

For some reason I was suddenly reminded of our room in Cannes, and Luc at the window saying: 'After you've had a bath and a good drink of whisky you'll feel better.' It was the first day, and I wasn't very happy; there were fourteen other days to come, fourteen days and nights with Luc. That was what I most desired at this very moment, and it would probably never happen again. If I had only known . . . but even if I had known, nothing would have been changed. Proust once wrote: 'It is very rare for happiness to be achieved at the exact moment it is desired.' It had happened to me that night: when I was with Luc, after longing for him all the week, my happiness was so intense that it made me quite ill. Perhaps this was due to the sudden ending of the emptiness that was my usual life. This emptiness had made me conscious that my life was cut in half, whereas the culmination of my happiness gave me the feeling that the divided halves and myself had at that moment joined together.

'Françoise,' called Pierre behind us. We turned round and exchanged partners. I found myself in front with Luc, walking in step along the red-paved avenue, and we must have had the same thought, for he gave me a questioning, almost a hard look.

'Well: yes,' I said.

He shrugged his shoulders resignedly, and raised his eyebrows. He took out a cigarette, lit it as he walked, and handed it to me.

Each time something upset him this was his resource. And yet he was a man completely devoid of habits.

'That fellow knows about us,' he said.

He spoke pensively, and without obvious apprehension.

'Is it serious?'

'He's not likely to resist the possibility of consoling Françoise. But I don't think his consoling her will necessarily lead to much.'

I admired the self-confidence of the male.

'He's rather a silly ass,' he said, 'an old college friend of Françoise's. You know what I mean?'

I knew.

He added: 'I am worried because it will hurt Françoise. The fact that you are involved . . .'

'Of course,' I said.

'I would regret it for your sake if Françoise felt badly about the part you played. She could do you a lot of good, you know, and she's a friend you can depend on.'

'I have no dependable friend,' I said sadly. 'I have nothing I can depend on.'

'Unhappy?' he asked, and he took my hand.

I was moved by his gesture and the evident risk he was running. He was holding my hand as we walked together under Françoise's very eye, but then she knew it was only Luc, a tired man, who held my hand. Probably she thought that if he had a bad conscience he would not have done it. He was not taking much of a risk. He was a man who did not care about anything. I pressed his hand; here he was with me; I never ceased to be astonished that my days should be filled with the thought of him, and only him.

'I'm not sad,' I answered, 'not at all.'

I lied. I would have liked to tell him that I was unhappy and that I really needed him. But when I was with him, it all seemed unreal. For in truth there was nothing; there had been nothing but those fifteen enjoyable days, my reveries, and my regrets. Why then was I so tortured? That was love's painful mystery, I thought derisively. But in fact I was annoyed with myself, because I knew that I was strong enough, free enough, and gifted enough to have a happy love affair.

Lunch lasted a long time. I watched Luc anxiously. He was so handsome and intelligent and tired; I did not want to lose him. I made vague plans for the winter. As he left he told me he would ring me up. Françoise added that she too would telephone to arrange to take me somewhere to see someone.

I did not hear from either of them for ten days. I could hardly bear to think of Luc. At last he telephoned to say that Françoise knew everything and he would get in touch with me as soon as he could, but he was overwhelmed with work. His voice was gentle. I remained perfectly still in my room, unable fully to take it in. I was going to have dinner with Alain. He could do nothing for me. My world was in ruins.

I saw Luc twice during the next fortnight, once in the bar in the Quai Voltaire, and then in a room, where we found nothing to say to each other, either before or afterwards. Everything had turned to dust and ashes. I realized that I was not suited to be the gay paramour of a married man. I loved him. I should have thought of that sooner, or at least have taken it into consideration; the obsession that is love, the agony when it is not satisfied. I tried to laugh. He did not reply. He spoke sweetly and tenderly, as if he were about to die. Françoise had been very unhappy.

He asked me what I was doing with myself. I told him I was working and reading. I read with the object of telling him about the book I was reading, or went to the cinema to see a film he once told me had been directed by a friend of his. I sought desperately for bonds between us, something apart from the sordid pain we had inflicted on Françoise, but there was nothing, not even remorse. I could not say to him: 'Do you remember?' It would have seemed like cheating, and would have alarmed him. I could not tell him that I saw, or thought I saw his car everywhere in the streets, that I constantly began to dial his number and never completed it, that I feverishly questioned my landlady every time I came in, that everything centred upon him, and that I hated myself so much I wanted to die. I had no right to tell him any of these things, no right even to his face, his hands, his gentle voice, nor to any of the unbearable past . . . I was getting thinner.

Alain was kind, so one day I told him everything. We were out for a long walk and he discussed my passion as if it were something in a book. This helped me to see it and speak of it objectively.

'You know perfectly well that it will end some time. In six months or a year you'll be able to joke about it.'

'I don't want to,' I said. 'It is not only a question of myself, it is all we were to each other; Cannes, our laughter, our understanding.'

'But that doesn't prevent your knowing that one day it won't matter any more.'

'I know it, but can't yet believe it. Anyhow, it is the present that matters, now, this very moment.'

We walked on and on. In the evening he came back with me as far as the pension and solemnly shook my hand. When I went in I asked the landlady if Monsieur Luc H. had telephoned. She said 'No' and smiled. I lay on my bed and thought of Cannes. I told myself: Luc doesn't love me; and it gave me a dull, sickly pain in my heart. I repeated it, and the pain came back more sharply. It seemed to me that I had made a discovery: from the fact that the pain was, so to speak, at my disposal and, armed to the teeth, was ready faithfully to answer my call, I could order it at will. I said: 'Luc doesn't love me,' and this astonishing thing happened. But even if I could turn the pain on and off as it suited me, I could not prevent it returning suddenly during a lecture or lunch, where it would attack and hurt me. I could do nothing about the misery of every day, my larva-like existence in the rain, feeling tired in the mornings, tedious lectures and conversations. I was suffering. I repeated the word to myself with curiosity, irony, anything that would cover up the sad evidence of an unhappy love.

What had to happen did happen. I met Luc again one evening. We drove through the Bois in his car. He told me he had to go to America for a month. I said 'how interesting,' then I suddenly realized: a whole month! I reached for a cigarette.

'When I get back, you'll have forgotten me,' he said.

'Why?' I asked.

'My poor darling, it would be better for you, so much better,' and he stopped the car.

I looked at his face. It was tense and sad. So he knew. He knew everything! He wasn't just a man one had to humour, he was also a friend. I clung to him all of a sudden. I laid my cheek against his. I stared out at the dark trees and I heard myself say the most incredible things:

'Luc, it mustn't happen. You can't leave me. I can't live without you. You must stay here. I'm so lonely, so dreadfully lonely, it is unbearable.'

I listened with surprise to my own voice. It was unashamed, youthful, supplicating. I told myself all the things Luc would say: 'There, there, you'll get over it, calm yourself,' but nevertheless I continued talking and Luc remained silent.

At last, as if to stop the flood of words, he took my head between his hands and gently kissed my mouth:

'My poor darling,' he said, 'my poor sweet!'

He spoke in a broken voice. I thought: 'so the time has come' and 'I'm really to be pitied,' and I began to cry against his waist-coat. Time was passing, and he would soon take me back to the house, exhausted. I would do nothing to stop him, and afterwards he would be gone. No! I couldn't allow it. 'No!' I said aloud.

I hung on to him. I would have liked to be him, to disappear.

'I'll telephone to you. I'll see you again before I leave,' he said. 'I'm so sorry, darling, so sorry. I was very happy with you. It will all pass, you know. Everything passes. I would give anything to . . .' He made a helpless gesture.

'To love me?' I said.

'Yes.'

His cheek was soft and warm with my tears. I was not going to see him for a month, he did not love me. How strange it was, this despair, and strange that one should ever recover from it. He took me back to the house. I had stopped crying. I was tired out. He telephoned the next day, and the one after. I had influenza the day he left. He came up for a moment to see me. Alain had just dropped in, and Luc kissed my cheek. He would write, he said.

15

Sometimes I woke in the night with a dry mouth, and before I had fully emerged from sleep something told me to lose myself once more in the warmth and unconsciousness which was my only refuge. But it was no use. I was already aware of my thirst and must get up and go to the wash-basin for a drink of water. When I saw my reflection in the glass by the dim light of the street lamp, and the tepid water was trickling down my throat, I was seized by a feeling of despair like a violent pain, and crept back to bed shivering. But I could not sleep, and the battle began. My memory and my imagination became two ferocious enemies. There was Luc's face, Cannes, what had been and what might have been, my body which needed sleep, and my mind which forbade it. I roused myself, sat up, and tried to reason it out: I loved Luc, who did not love me, therefore I was bound to suffer, and the only remedy was to break it off. I thought of ways of doing this: for instance, writing him a well-phrased, noble letter, explaining that all was over between us, but I found I was only interested in concocting a beautifully expressed letter that would be bound to bring Luc back to me. And no sooner did I imagine myself cruelly separated from him than I began to think about our reconciliation.

People always say one should control one's passions. But for whose sake should I do so? I was not interested in anyone else, nor in myself, except in so far as my relationship with Luc was affected.

206

I thought of Alain, Catherine, the streets, a boy who had kissed me at an impromptu party, whom I never wished to see again, the rain, the Sorbonne, cafés, maps of America (I hated America), my boredom; would it never end? It was more than a month since Luc had left. I had received one sad, tender little note from him that I knew by heart.

My one comfort was that my intellect, until then opposed to this passion, always mocking me and trying to make me feel ridiculous, leading me into violent arguments with myself, was gradually becoming more of an ally. I no longer said to myself: 'Let's put a stop to all this nonsense,' but 'How can I find a way out of my unhappiness?' Each night saw the same dreary repetition, but the days sometimes passed quickly, with lectures to occupy me. I tried to think of Luc and myself as if we were a 'case', but there were terrible moments when I stopped dead on the pavement with a feeling of rage and disgust. I would go into a café, slip twenty francs into the juke-box, and give myself five minutes' pleasure listening to the tune we had heard in Cannes. Alain began to hate it, but I knew every note. It reminded me of the scent of mimosa, and altogether gave me my money's worth. I did not like myself.

'Try to be calm, my dear!' said Alain, patient as ever.

I did not usually like being called 'my dear', but in this case it was rather a comfort.

'You are very kind,' I said.

'Not at all,' he would reply. 'I shall write my thesis on the subject of passion. It interests me.'

But the music finally convinced me that Luc was necessary to me. I knew very well that my need of him was both part of, and separated from, my love. I was still capable of disassociating in him the human being, the accessory, and the object of my passion: the enemy. The worst was not being able to despise him a little, as one usually does those who are only lukewarm towards one. There were also moments when I said to myself: 'Poor Luc, what a bore and a nuisance I would be to him!' and I reproached myself for not having taken our affair lightly, all the more as it might have attached him to me out of pique. But I knew very well he was incapable of such feelings. He wasn't an adversary, he was Luc. And so I went on and on.

One day, when I was just leaving my room at two o'clock to go to a lecture, I was called to the telephone. My heart no longer missed a beat as I answered it, because Luc was away. I heard Françoise's low, hesitating voice:

'Dominique?'

'Yes,' I answered.

There was absolute stillness on the staircase.

'Dominique, I meant to telephone to you before. Will you come and see me all the same?'

'Of course,' I said. I had my voice so much under control that it must have sounded quite artificial.

'Would you like to come this evening at six o'clock?'

'Very well.'

She hung up.

I was both upset and pleased to hear her voice. It brought back our week-ends, the car, lunches in restaurants, a whole way of life.

16

I did not go to my lecture. I walked about the streets and wondered what she could have to say to me. Considering what I had already been through, it seemed to me that nothing could hurt me much. At six o'clock it was raining a little; the roads were damp and shiny under the lights, like the back of a seal. Coming into the house I saw myself in the looking-glass. I had grown very much thinner, and I vaguely hoped to fall dangerously ill and that Luc would come and sob at my bedside while I lay dying. My hair was wet and I looked hunted. I should appeal to Françoise's boundless kindness. I stayed a moment longer in front of the glass. Perhaps I should have tried to attach Françoise to me, plotted with Luc, and been more artful, but how could I do anything of the sort when my feelings were so deeply involved? I had been surprised at the force of my love and admired myself for it, but I had forgotten that it represented nothing for me except a chance to suffer.

Françoise opened the door with a half-smile, looking rather frightened. I took off my waterproof as I came in.

'Are you well?' I asked.

'Very well,' she said. 'Do sit down.'

She said 'vous'; I had forgotten that she used to call me 'tu'. I sat down. She looked at me, visibly amazed at my lamentable appearance, which made me feel sorry for myself.

'Will you have something to drink?'

'Yes, please.'

She fetched some whisky. I had forgotten the taste. I thought of my depressing room, the university restaurant, and the rust-coloured coat they had given me which had served me well. I felt strained and desperate, almost sure of myself, through my exasperation.

'Well, there we are!' I said.

I raised my eyes and looked at her. She was sitting on the divan opposite, staring fixedly at me; without a word. We might still talk of other things, and I could say to her on leaving, looking very embarrassed: 'I hope you are not too angry with me?' It depended on me; it would be sufficient to talk quickly before our silence became a double confession. But I was silent. The moment had come; I was living through it.

'I should have liked to telephone you sooner,' she said at last, 'because Luc asked me to, and also because I was sorry that you were alone in Paris, but . . .'

'I too ought to have rung you up,' I said.

'Why?'

I was going to say: 'to make my excuses', but the words seemed feeble. I began to tell the truth.

'Because I wanted to, because I felt very lonely, because I hated to think that you thought . . .'

I made a vague gesture.

'You look ill,' she said kindly.

'Yes,' I said resentfully. 'If it had been possible, I would have come to see you; you would have made me eat beefsteaks, I should have lain on your carpet, you would have comforted me. By ill-luck, you were the only person who could have helped me, and the only one I could not ask.'

I trembled, my hand shook. Françoise's gaze became unbearable. She took the glass away, put it on the table, and sat down again.

'I was jealous,' she said quietly. 'I was physically jealous.'

I was dumbfounded. I expected anything but that.

'It was stupid,' she said. 'I knew quite well that you and Luc . . . it wasn't serious.'

When she saw my expression she made a gesture as though excusing herself, which seemed to me admirable.

'I mean,' she said, 'that physical infidelity is not really important; but I was always like that, and now still more, now that . . .'

She seemed to be suffering, and I was afraid of what she was going to say.

'Now that I am not so young,' she finished, and, turning her head away, 'less desirable.'

'No,' I said.

I protested. I had not thought this story could have another dimension, unknown to me, ordinary, sad, perhaps pitiable. I had believed it was my story; but I knew nothing of their life.

'It was not that,' I said, and got up.

I went towards her and remained standing. She turned round and smiled at me a little.

'My poor little Dominique,' she said. 'What a muddle.'

I sat down next to her and held my head in my hands. My ears were buzzing. I felt empty. I would have liked to cry.

'I like you very much,' she said. 'I don't like to think you have been unhappy. When I saw you the first time I thought we could give you a happier expression instead of that beaten look you had. It was not very successful.'

'I have been a little unhappy,' I said, 'but then Luc warned me.'

I would have liked to melt against her large, generous body, to tell her that I wished she had been my mother, that I was very unhappy; and to whimper. But now I could not even do that.

'He returns in ten days,' she said.

Did I still feel a shock? But Françoise must have Luc and her semi-happiness. I must sacrifice myself. This thought made me smile. It was the last effort to hide my unimportance. I had nothing to sacifice, no hope. I had only to put an end, or let time put an end, to an illness. This bitter resignation was not wholly devoid of optimism.

'Later, when it is all over, I hope to see you again, Françoise, and Luc too. Now there is nothing to do but wait.'

On the threshold she kissed me gently.

'Well, I shall see you soon.'

When I got home I fell on my bed. What had I said to her? What cold rubbish! Luc will come back. He will take me in his arms and kiss me. Even if he doesn't love me, he will be there, and this nightmare will be over.

After ten days Luc returned. I knew it because I passed his house in a bus the day of his arrival, and saw his car. I went back to the pension and waited for his telephone call. It did not come. Neither that day, nor the next, and I remained in bed to wait for it, pretending I had influenza.

He was there and he had not rung me up. After a month and a half's absence! My shivering, half-hysterical laughter and obsessive apathy all added up to one thing – despair. I had never suffered so much. I said to myself: this is the last blow, and the hardest!

The third day I got up and went to my lectures. Alain walked with me again. I listened attentively to all he said. I laughed. Without knowing why, I was haunted by a certain phrase:

'Something is rotten in the state of Denmark!'

I kept repeating it.

The fifteenth day I woke to hear music in the courtyard coming from a kind neighbour's radio. It was a beautiful Andante by Mozart, as always evoking the dawn, death, and a certain way of smiling. I listened to it for some time, motionless in my bed. I felt rather happy.

The landlady called me. I was wanted on the telephone. I put on my dressing-gown without hurrying and went downstairs. I thought it must be Luc, and that it was no longer very important.

'How are you?'

I heard his voice. It was his voice, but whence came that feeling of calm, of peace? Something in me had changed. He asked me to have a drink with him the following day. 'Yes, yes,' I said.

I went up to my room very thoughtfully. The music had ceased, and I regretted having missed the end. I was surprised to see myself smile in the glass. I did not stop myself smiling, I could not. Once more, I knew it, I was alone. I wanted to repeat that word to myself: alone, alone. But what of it? I was a woman, and I had loved a man. It was a simple story; there was nothing to make a fuss about.

PENGUIN MODERN CLASSICS

WIDE SARGASSO SEA
JEAN RHYS

'Rhys took one of the works of genius of the nineteenth century and turned it inside-out to create one of the works of genius of the twentieth century'
Michèle Roberts, *The Times*

Jean Rhys's late literary masterpiece, *Wide Sargasso Sea*, was inspired by Charlotte Brontë's *Jane Eyre*, and is set in the lush, beguiling landscape of Jamaica in the 1830s.

Born into an oppressive colonialist society, Creole heiress Antoinette Cosway meets a young Englishman who is drawn to her innocent sensuality and beauty. After their marriage, disturbing rumours begin to circulate, poisoning her husband against her. Caught between his demands and her own precarious sense of belonging, Antoinette is driven towards madness.

PENGUIN MODERN CLASSICS

MRS DALLOWAY
VIRGINIA WOOLF

Clarissa Dalloway, elegant and vivacious, is preparing for a party and remembering those she once loved. In another part of London, Septimus Warren Smith is shell-shocked and on the brink of madness. Smith's day interweaves with that of Clarissa and her friends, their lives converging as the party reaches its glittering climax.

Past, present and future are brought together one momentous June day in 1923.

Edited by Stella McNichol
With an Introduction and Notes by Elaine Showalter

PENGUIN MODERN CLASSICS

A SPY IN THE HOUSE OF LOVE
ANAÏS NIN

'Her sense of woman is unique … she excites male readers and incites female readers' *The New York Times*

Sabina is a firebird blazing through 1950s New York: she is a woman daring to enjoy the sexual licence that men have always known. Wearing extravagant outfits and playing dangerous games of desire, she deliberately avoids commitment, gripped by the pursuit of pleasure for its own sake.

In *A Spy in the House of Love*, Anaïs Nin expressed her individual vision of feminine sexuality with a ferocious dramatic force. Through Sabina's affairs with four men, she lays bare all the duplicity and fragmentation of self involved in the search for love.

Contemporary ... Provocative ... Outrageous ...
Prophetic ... Groundbreaking ... Funny ... Disturbing ...
Different ... Moving ... Revolutionary ... Inspiring ...
Subversive ... Life-changing ...

What makes a modern classic?

At Penguin Classics our mission has always been to make the best
books ever written available to everyone. And that also means
constantly redefining and refreshing exactly what makes a 'classic'.
That's where Modern Classics come in. Since 1961 they have been an
organic, ever-growing and ever-evolving list of books from the last
hundred (or so) years that we believe will continue to be read over and
over again.

They could be books that have inspired political dissent, such as
Animal Farm. Some, like *Lolita* or *A Clockwork Orange*, may have
caused shock and outrage. Many have led to great films, from *In Cold
Blood* to *One Flew Over the Cuckoo's Nest*. They have broken down
barriers – whether social, sexual, or, in the case of *Ulysses*, the
boundaries of language itself. And they might – like *Goldfinger* or
Scoop – just be pure classic escapism. Whatever the reason, Penguin
Modern Classics continue to inspire, entertain and enlighten millions
of readers everywhere.

'No publisher has had more influence on reading habits than Penguin'
Independent

'Penguins provided a crash course in world literature'
Guardian

The best books ever written

PENGUIN CLASSICS

SINCE 1946

Find out more at www.penguinclassics.com